The Moths
and Other Stories

Helena María Viramontes

Arte Público Press
Houston, Texas
1995

Stories in this collection have previously appeared in the following publications: "Growing" in *Cuentos: Stories by Latinas*; "The Moths" in *201: Homenaje a la Ciudad de Los Angeles, XhismArte Magazine*; "Birthday" in *Cenzontle: Chicano Short Stories and Poetry*; "Broken Web" in *Statement Magazine* and *Woman of Her Word*; The Long Reconciliation" in *XhismArte Magazine*; and "Snapshots" in *Maize*.

Recovering the past, creating the future

Arte Público Press
University of Houston
452 Cullen Performance Hall
Houston, Texas 77204-2004

Cover design by Mark Piñón
Original art "La Butterfly"
by John Valadez, 1983

Library of Congress Catalog Number 84-072308
ISBN 1-55885-138-0

The paper used in this publication meets the requirements of the American National Standard for Permanence of Paper for Printed Library Materials Z39.48-1984. ∞

Second Printing, 1988
Third Printing, 1991
Fourth Printing, 1992
Second Edition, 1995

2 3 4 5 6 7 8 9 0 1   13 12 11 10 9 8 7 6

Contents

Introduction, by Yvonne Yarbo-Bejarano 9

The Moths 27

Growing 35

Birthday 45

The Broken Web 53

The Cariboo Cafe 65

The Long Reconciliation 83

Snapshots 99

Neighbors 109

To Mary Louise Labrada Viramontes
for Pilar

Introduction

Introduction

With this collection of stories, Helena María Viramontes makes an important contribution to the growing body of writing by Chicanas and Latinas in this country whose art speaks to the reality of women of color. It has been apparent for some time that Chicanas are riding a wave of creative expression that is carrying them to the forefront in the field of literary creativity in the United States. This trend has been most visible in the area of poetry, where a veritable explosion of Chicanas' creative energies has occurred. Chicanas have moved more recently into fiction, as witnessed by Lucha Corpi's prize-winning entry in the University of Texas at El Paso's short-story contest "Palabra Nueva," the publication of Gina Valdés' novel *There Are No Madmen Here* (San Diego: Maize Press, 1981), and the stories represented in the collection *Woman of Her Word: Hispanic Women Write* (Houston: Arte Publico Press, 1983), edited by Evangelina Vigil, to mention a few achievements among many.

The current effervescence of Chicana writers is a tribute to their strength and determination to be heard, given the nature of the obstacles which lie in their path. The Chicana writers share with all women writers the problem of breaking into a male-dominated industry, but they must overcome others related to class and race as well. A long history of economic, racial and linguistic oppression has relegated the Chicana to menial jobs, systematically denied her access to literacy and robbed her of her mother tongue when she succeeds in educating herself. Even when she does learn to write, the self-hatred and sense of inferiority indoctrinated in all women by a patriarchal system of values, and exaggerated in the Chicana by her color and her class, militate against her conviction that she has something worth saying. In her open letter to third-world women writers, Gloria Anzaldúa suggests that their real struggle involves the search for a voice which is uniquely theirs. The Chicana writer must draw strength from the very conditions seen as sources of inferiority by the oppressor: her sex, her race and culture, her class. The search for their authentic voice has led Chicana writers to explore the personal in relationship to a collective identity. This process is not just one of affirmation, but also one of questioning and critical examination. At the same time that the Chicana writer recognizes her collective and familial history as a source of strength, she challenges values which continue to oppress women within the Chicano family and culture.

This brings me to the importance of the stories published in this collection, stories written by a Chicana about women of all ages. Viramontes does not present idealized versions of feminists successfully battling patriarchy. Acutely aware of women's dilemmas, Viramontes creates female characters who are a contradictory blend of strengths and weaknesses, struggling against lives of unfulfilled potential and restrictions forced upon them because of their sex. These women are conscious that something is wrong with their lives, and that what is wrong is linked to the rigid gender roles imposed on them by their men and their culture, often with the aid of the Church. Most display resistance: the rebellious behavior of the adolescents in "Growing" and "The Moths," the courageous decision to abort taken by Alice in "Birthday" and Amanda in "The Long Reconciliation," and the perpetration of criminal violence in "The Broken Web."

Viramontes focuses her narrative lens on the struggles of women within the Chicano family and culture, although larger social and economic conflicts often form a backdrop or frame for the main action. The relationship between Chato and Amanda in "The Long Reconciliation" is only understandable in light of the crushing poverty and exploitation of their lives in Mexico. In "The Broken Web," Tomás transports undocumented workers into the United States to work in the fields where he himself, his wife and his three children slave under the Fresno sun during the grape harvest. "Neighbors" captures the desperation of the *barrio*, where "tough-minded boy-men" gather in groups to drink and "lose themselves in the abyss of defeat," locked out of the dominant society by economic factors and discriminatory attitudes as effective as padlocks. Fierro is killed by the "heartaches" of losing a son to

senseless violence and forty years of memories to the free-
ways which obliterated his home in the *barrio* "with clawing
efficiency." In the same story, Aura unleashes a chain of
events which demonstrate the reality of police harrassment in
the *barrio*. The disproportionate number of patrol cars, the
flashing of red lights, and the batons speak of the brutality
and prejudice which permeate the characters' lives. When the
police subdue a youth who tries to escape, Aura hears "the
creak of their thick leather belts rubbing against their bullets."

But racial prejudice and the economic and social oppression of Chicanos in this country are rarely the central theme
of these stories. Viramontes is concerned primarily with the
social and cultural values which shape women's lives and
against which they struggle with varying degrees of success.
Most of the stories develop a conflict between a female character and the man who represents the maximum authority in
her life, either father or husband. The fathers in "Growing"
and "Moths" are oppressive figures who threaten violence and
demand obedient acceptance of traditional roles. In "Growing," Naomi is bewildered by her father's distrust of her, not
fully realizing that this distrust is inherent in her culture's
definition of gender:

> It was Apá who refused to trust her, and she could not
> understand what she had done to make him so distrustful.
> *TÚ ERES MUJER*, he thundered, and that was the end of
> any argument, any question, and the matter was closed
> because he said those three words as if they were a con-
> demnation from the heavens and so she couldn't be
> trusted.

In many cases, Viramontes shows the collusion of the
Catholic Church in the socialization of women in rigid gender
roles. In "The Moths," the father's violent opposition to his
adolescent daughter's deviation from the cultural norm of
femininity is closely linked to her rejection of the Church:

> That was one of Apá's biggest complaints. He would pound
> his hands on the table, rocking the sugar dish or spilling a
> cup of coffee and scream that if I didn't go to Mass every
> Sunday to save my goddam sinning soul, then I had no rea-
> son to go out of the house, period. Punto final. He would
> grab my arm and dig his nails into me to make sure I

understood the importance of catechism. Did he make himself clear?

To assume more independence and responsibility in their
lives, the women in these stories must break with years of
indoctrination by the Church. In "Birthday," Alice's decision
to take control of her own body and future by having an abortion is accompanied not only by guilt but by a radical redefini-
tion of her relationship to her religion as well. After listening
to Alice rationalize her position, her friend Terry responds:
"Look, you'll stew and brood and feel pitiful and pray until
your knees chap—but in the end you'll decide on the abortion.
So why not cut out this silliness?" At the end, Alice reveals
her contradictory feelings, mixing expressions of guilt ("forgive me for I have sinned") with rejections of God ("No! I don't
love you, not you, God") and loss of self-esteem ("not even
me"). In "The Long Reconciliation," Amanda decides to abort
because she cannot bear "to watch a child slowly rot," defying
the values of her community and her husband and the dic-
tates of the priest: "It is so hard being female, Amanda, and
you must understand that that is the way it was meant to
be...." She reveals her disillusionment with a distant God who
does not help the poor: "But, Father, wasn't He supposed to
take care of us, His poor?... You, God, eating and drinking as
you like, you, there, not feeling the sweat or the pests that
feed on the skin, you sitting with a kingly lust for comfort, tell
us that we will be paid later on in death." In "The Broken
Web," Martha reveals the trauma of her father's murder to
the priest through the language of a dream in which she identifies her father with a statue of Christ which shatters into
little pieces. As Evangelina Vigil points out in her introduction to the collection *Woman of Her Word*, the priest "is
detached from the spiritual needs of those he confesses" (p.
11). The mother in the same story expresses her guilt at
killing her husband and her sense of alienation from a male,
authoritarian God: "Her children in time would forgive her.
But God? He would never understand. He was a man, too."

In most cases, Viramontes' female characters pay dearly
for breaking with traditional values concerning women, and
the exploration of their sexuality often brings negative consequences.

In "Birthday," Alice's fear of the abortion is only partly due to her religious upbringing; she is also frightened of having to make the decision. Characterized as a child in the story, Alice looks for direction first to her shadowy boyfriend, then to Terry. She realizes that having to make the decision alone is both burdensome and liberating. Accepting responsibility for her life matures and empowers her. When her boyfriend tells her it was her responsibility not to get pregnant, "her eyes, that had first pleaded desperately under the tree, now looked upon him as a frightened child." The positive exploration of her sexuality, expressed in the poetic passage which opens and closes the story, is negatively tinged with guilt and the trauma of the abortion: "No sex, Alice. Punishing me. For loving? God! Fucking, Alice...God isn't pregnant, Alice." At the end, the passage of ecstatic sublimation is invaded by guilt ("forgive me, Father, for I have sinned"), juxtaposing pleasure ("God, how I love it"), rejection of God ("No! I don't love you, not you, God") and the "cold hands" in her experience of the abortion.

Aura, the old female character in "Neighbors," leads an isolated and solitary existence. The arrival of the strange woman disrupts the silent bond which she has formed with Fierro, her old neighbor, and heightens Aura's solitude. She spies on them, envious of their laughing and dancing to a tune which takes her back to her youth. She goes to bed after watching them, "cold under the bleached, white sheets." At first she attributes her feelings of weakness and uneasiness to the medication she was taking during her illness, but realizes the hollowness in her stomach is caused by the presence of the strange woman: "Aura's heart sank like an anchor into an ocean of silence." The youths of the neighborhood take their revenge on Aura for making the mistake of calling the police; she decides that since she is totally alone she must take care of herself. She gets the gun and sits with it facing the door, terrified, "because she refused to be helpless." Her mind goes back to the rattlers her grandfather taught her how to kill, which she identifies with what is "out there" menacing her: the youths who have sworn to "get her," but also the stranger who has disrupted the pattern of her existence. Ironically, Aura's refusal to be passive leads to the armed confrontation, not with Rubén or Toastie, but with the strange

woman who has destroyed the one tenuous relationship Aura
has with her "neighbors."

Olga Ruiz, in "Snapshots," is a middle-aged woman who
has been trapped by the meaningless routines of a wasted life.
She has spent thirty years in total self-abnegation, trying to
fulfill the role of perfect wife and mother. The gap between
the ideal and her reality is captured by the "snapshot": "If it
wasn't for the burnt cupcakes, my damn varicose veins, and
Marge blubbering all over her day suit, it would have made a
perfect snapshot for him to keep." Hers is a story of unfulfill-
ment, having dissipated her life in the hopeless pursuit of
cleanliness:

> How can people believe that for years I've fought against
> motes of dust and dirt-attracting floors or bleached white
> sheets to perfection when a few hours later the motes, the
> dirt, the stains return to remind me of the uselessness of it
> all? I was always too busy to listen to swans slicing the
> lake water or watch the fluttering wings of wild geese fly-
> ing south for a warm winter. I missed the heartbeat I could
> have heard if I had just held Marge a little closer.

Her divorce and her alienation from her daughter have opened
her eyes to the time she has lost. She rebels, letting the dust
collect under the bed, "as it should be." But she substitutes her
previous frenzy of meaningless activity with non-activity, not
with productive action: "To be quite frank, the fact of the matter is I wish to do nothing but allow indolence to rush through
my veins with frightening speed." Olga Ruiz describes her
obsession with the albums of snapshots as an addiction to nostalgia and searches them for lost time, for the past that never
existed which has taken away her future. The snapshots are
ghosts she can no longer recognize; she herself has "faded into
thirty years of trivia." The distance and lack of affection
between her parents, between her and her parents, and
between her and her daughter is mirrored in her attitude
toward her sexuality. She viewed sex as something to be done
privately and efficiently, not necessarily for pleasure, and
when her husband searched her eyes the next morning, she
says she "never could figure out what he expected to find
there." She desperately searches for meaning in the snapshots,
yet knows they are unreal, frozen moments of time. Olga
wishes Marge would "jump out of any snapshot," break out of

their programmed patterns of relating as mother and daughter. She fears that Marge is turning into another "Olga," blending into nothing. Her panic over losing her identity drives her to the snapshots, but she is equally horrified by what they reveal. The story ends with her torn between her rejection of the snapshots and her need for them: "It scares me to think that my grandmother may have been right. It scares me even more to think I don't have a snapshot of her. So, I'll go through my album, and if I find one, I'll tear it up for sure."

In "The Long Reconciliation," Amanda is almost a child when she marries. She is considered wild by her family, "like the jackrabbits, timid, not strong, but strong-willed." After discovering her sexuality on her wedding night, Amanda has come to think of sex as one of the only pleasures in her life. The priest tries to force her to accept sex only for procreation, but she refuses to give it up: "Sex is the only free pleasure we have. It makes us feel like clouds for the minutes that not even you can prevent. You ask us not to lie together, but we are not made of you, we are not gods." She experiences pregnancy as a threat to her meager survival resources: "To awake and feel something inside draining you. Lying on my back, I can almost see where all my energy is going....I stroke it to calm its vulgar hunger, but it won't be satisfied until it gets all of me." Her defiance of the taboo against abortion costs her the love of her husband Chato and the expression of her sexuality. After the abortion, Chato shuns her, rejecting her attempts "to make him love her again. Each time she touched him, he saw his child's face and would jerk away from her grasp." Her affair with Don Joaquín, the hated landowner who has sold Chato a piece of worthless land, causes her great sadness and guilt because she still loves Chato and longs for him to forgive her. She ends the affair too late, for Chato finds out about it and stabs Don Joaquín. Amanda herself takes a savage revenge on her ex-lover for telling her husband, ripping open his wound and stuffing it with maggots to hasten his death. Chato is unable to forgive Amanda, accusing her of acting like God by daring to change their destiny and insisting that in killing Don Joaquín he acted like a man should. When he tells her that he has killed for honor, Amanda replies that he acted in blind obedience to his concept of his role as a man:

...I killed for life....Which is worse? You killed because something said, "you must kill to remain a man."...For me,
things are as different as our bodies....But you couldn't
understand that because something said, "you must have
sons to remain a man."

The carousel represents Chato's dreams for the future,
dreams dashed by the poverty of the land, the oppression of
Don Joaquín and Amanda's decision to abort their son. The
difference between Chato and Amanda is captured in the
scene where he attempts to console her, not realizing that her
anguish is caused by her pregnancy:

She heard him fumbling through some boxes in the closet
and turned to find him holding the carousel. "Children die
like crops here," she said, but he could not hear her for the
bells of carousel music came forth sounding like an orchestra in the silence of the night.

Chato leaves and goes north, where he finally makes his
peace with Amanda as he lies dying many years later in a
hospital. He refers to his withholding of forgiveness as a
mountain "too big for two little hands, one closed heart, too
immovable." Only at the end does he realize "that the mountain was no bigger than a stone, a stone I could have thrown
into the distance where the earth and sky meet, thrown it
away at 24 but instead waited 58 years...." Amanda helps him
"cast the stone," initiating the "long reconciliation" of the title.
But this forgiveness is tinged with bitter fatalism. Chato realizes the futility of his dreams ("the carousel horse with a
glossy silver saddle moving but going nowhere was just
wood") and of his life: "Maybe we were all born cheated. There
is no justice, only honor in that little world out in the desert
where our house sits like decayed bones. All that can be done
is what you have done, Amanda; sit on the porch and weave
your threads into time."

    The nameless female character of "The Broken Web" suf-
fers the worst consequence for her violent break with the traditional role imposed on women. As Vigil points out, she is
weighed down by her subservience to Tomás and the respon-
siblity of her family, and she acts to free herself "from the
misery...of guilt imposed by man and God" (pp. 12-13). Musing
on the fate of Olivia, the aging barmaid, she wonders if she
would become like her if Tomás left her. By murdering

Tomás, the woman breaks the cycle of use and abuse, just as she breaks the web of the title which connects the different women in the story through Tomás. Speaking to the dead man "with the voice of prayer," the woman explains how she has been "tired and wrinkled and torn by him, his God, his word." Her sexuality as well as her individuality have been stifled by their marriage. She tells Tomás that she gave up being a woman when she married him, and earlier in the story she thinks that "only in complete solitude did she feel like a woman." Before marrying Tomás, she had defied the rules governing women's behavior by sleeping with another man. But this had only increased her oppression, fueling Tomás' rage against her. She feels enslaved by her marriage and her children: "And she could not leave him because she no longer owned herself. He owned her, her children owned her, and she needed them all to live. And she was tired of needing." But her act of liberation from this life of imprisonment results in literal incarceration, and even after killing Tomás, she is not released from his power over her. Dead, he seems more alive to her, "more real than anything, anyone around her." She herself feels "equally dead, but equally real." Dead, he is an "invincible cloud of past" whose blood "stained all tomorrows." She cannot escape Tomás by killing him; she believes she has condemned her soul to punishment. All she has left is the strength of defiant resignation, picturing herself as a "cricket wailing nightly for redemption."

"Neighbors" tells the story of an isolated old woman; "Snapshots," "The Broken Web," and "The Long Reconciliation" present women struggling with the limitations imposed on them by marriage. The two stories which open the collection, "Growing" and "Moths," deal with another phase of women's life cycle: the threshold of puberty.

"Growing" captures the pain and confusion of adolescence. Naomi rebels against social and cultural values which dictate how her life must change because her body has changed. The exploration of her budding sexuality either leads to punishment or is tied to restrictions on her behavior imposed by the male. When her relationship with Eloy turns sexual, he becomes jealous and excludes her from activities she used to share with the other children.

> There were too many demands on her, and no one showed
> her how to fulfill them, and wasn't it crazy?...and she began
> to act different because everyone began treating her differ-
> ent and wasn't it crazy? She could no longer be herself and
> her father could no longer trust her because she was a
> woman.

For her, becoming a "woman" is associated with loss of freedom and a vague sense of the oppression and injustice that
await her. Her loss is momentarily attenuated by a baseball
game. For a fleeting moment she returns to the world of childhood from which she has been barred. But her participation
in the game is, appropriately, from the sidelines; she is like
an outsider looking through a window at what was once hers
and is now irretrievably lost. At the end of the story she sees
her own lost childhood in her little sister's sleeping face and
envies her uncomplicated existence. The story is a lament for
the sexual innocence and the carefree play of childhood; for
Naomi, her newly discovered sexuality means only burdensome restrictions, frightening changes and confusing demands of conformity to her culture's definition of the woman's
role.

   "The Moths" links the painful experience of adolescence
with another threshold experience. The death of her abuela is
part of the rebellious tomboy's maturing process. She mourns
the loss of the only person who understood her, and weeps for
the death of her own childhood and innocence as well. Like
"Growing," "The Moths" shows the coercive socialization of
adolescent girls in femininity as defined by their culture. The
adolescent protagonist of the story is acutely aware that she
is "different" from her sisters:

> I wasn't even pretty or nice like my older sisters and I just
> couldn't do the girl things they could do. My hands were
> too big to handle the fineries of crocheting or embroidery
> and I always pricked my fingers or knotted my colored
> threads time and time again while my sisters laughed and
> called me "bull hands" with their cute waterlike voices.

The animosity created between her and her sisters by their
mockery of her difference explodes periodically in anger and
violence; she is beaten for this and for her disrespectful rebel-
liousness. As in the above quote, her feeling of being different
and awkward is concentrated in her hands: "My hands began

to fan out, grow like a liar's nose until they hung by my side like low weights." The grandmother reshapes her granddaughter's hands, returning their use to her and making her feel more comfortable with herself: "Abuelita made a balm out of dried moth wings and Vicks and rubbed my hands, shaped them back to size and it was the strangest feeling. Like bones melting. Like sun shining through the darkness of your eyelids." Her grandmother's house is a peaceful refuge from the stormy home environment of quarrels and beatings, an evocative world of calm vegetation in which she feels protected by her abuela's "gray eye" and comfortable silence: "It made me feel, in a strange sort of way, safe and guarded and not alone. Like God was supposed to make you feel." Since her grandmother had "melted and formed" her hands, she feels that it is "only fair" that the same hands be the ones to care for her abuela on her deathbed, rubbing her body, arms and legs. The rejection of the cold emptiness of the church, closely associated with her father, contrasts with her feelings of protected safety at her grandmother's: "I looked up at the high ceiling. I had forgotten the vastness of these places, the coolness of the marble pillars and the frozen statues with blank eyes. I knew why I had never returned." In the chapel she remembers her father's overbearing determination to indoctrinate her in her role as a woman through religion. Sent off to Mass, she would go to her abuela's instead, where one day, helping her make chile, she works out her feelings under the silent gaze of her grandmother:

> The chiles made my eyes water. Am I crying? No, Mama Luna, I'm sure not crying. I don't like going to Mass, but my eyes watered anyway, the tears dropping on the table cloth like candle wax...I...began to crush and crush and twist and crush the heart out of the tomato, the clove of garlic, the stupid chiles that made me cry, crushed them until they turned into liquid under my bull hand. With a wooden spoon, I scraped hard to destroy the guilt, and my tears were gone.

Unlike her relationship with her grandmother, her relationship with her mother is strained. Her sisters berate her for hurting their mother by being selfish, disrespectful and unbelieving. She feels distant from her mother's pain at losing her own mother and cannot comfort her. It is hard for her to express emotions other than anger. She is too tough and proud to admit to her grandmother that she is crying, and does not kiss either her abuela or her mother ("I never kissed her," she says, of both). She manages to give her mother a pat on the back, but she cannot refrain from telling her how the grandmother fell off the bed, although she herself does not understand why she wanted to say it: "I guess I became angry and just so tired of the quarrels and unanswered prayers and my hands hanging helplessly by my side." Hurt by her own inability to feel and express her feelings, she asks herself to give, when to stop and when to start. That she will learn is indicated by her regaining her hands once more: "and when my hands fell from my lap, I awoke to catch them." She finds her abuela dead: "She had turned to the window and tried to speak, but her mouth remained open and speechless." Through the mystery of death and the experience of mortal corruption, she begins to understand the miracle of rebirth, expressed in the image of the sun and her reassuring words to her dead grandmother: "'I heard you, Abuelita,' I said, stroking her cheek. 'I heard you.'" These words suggest that her grandmother has handed down something to her which will persist as a part of herself. She bathes her abuela's body in a cleansing ritual which is also a rite of passage. Her acceptance of death is accompanied by the poetic image of the title, the small gray moths which come from the abuela's soul and through her mouth, "fluttering to the light, circling the single dull bulb of the bathroom." She finally finds release in a flood of purging tears as she weeps for her grandmother, her mother and herself, "the sobs puking the hate from the depths of anguish, the misery of feeling half born, sobbing until finally the sobs rippled into circles and circles of sadness and relief."

In "The Cariboo Cafe," Viramontes reveals another facet of her social consciousness as a writer, one with which she has been increasingly concerned lately. "The Cariboo Cafe" places the conflict in Central America at the center of her narrative world. Broadening her thematic spectrum, Viramontes addresses the plight of women suffering under repressive regimes which rob them of their children. The story weaves three paths which intersect with fatal consequences. In the process, Viramontes shows the economic and social parallels between the woman from El Salvador and the children of

other "displaced people" in this country who live in fear of the
urban jungle and La Migra. The cook of the Cariboo Cafe
emerges as a fragmented consciousness from the shipwreck of
his life, shot through with the loneliness of losing wife and
son. He betrays the undocumented workers who seek refuge
from La Migra in his bathroom out of rage and frustration at
his own miserable existence. Although he justifies his action
to himself ("Now look, I'm a nice guy, but I don't like to be
used, you know? Just because they're regulars don't mean
jackshit"), he is left with the burning stare of the old woman
seared into his memory. He also betrays the woman and the
two children to the police. Ironically, his denunciation is moti-
vated by his belief that "children gotta be with their parents,
family gotta be together." Through the story of this woman—
from the morning her small son disappears to the day years
later in the United States when she clings to the desperate
delusion that she has found him once again—Viramontes
makes a strong statement about the every-day horror that
makes up the pattern of existence in countries like El Salvador.

"The Cariboo Cafe" is characteristic of Viramontes' narrative technique. In this story, as in others, she experiments
with shifting points of view, interweaving various characters'
perspectives and avoiding a linear development of the action.
"The Broken Web" and "The Long Reconciliation" make the
severest demands on readers' ability to reconstruct the tem-
poral sequence of events. The language of the stories is rich
and varied. Viramontes' style in "Snapshots" captures Olga
Ruiz's dilemma with an offhand humor that is both poignant
and wacky. The cook in "The Cariboo Cafe" is particularly
well-characterized through his speech. Ways of seeing and
speaking typical of children and adolescents make up the styl-
istic texture of "Growing," "Moths," and "The Cariboo Cafe,"
combined with an expressive density of poetic imagery. On
the whole, Viramontes' language is terse and innovative. Her
exploration of narrative structure and her constant struggle
with words to make them yield fresh insights constitute an
ongoing concern with craft in order to form a vehicle for these
women's stories that need to be told and heard.

Yvonne Yarbro-Bejarano
Stanford University

The Moths
and Other Stories

The Moths

The Moths

I was fourteen years old when Abuelita requested my help. And it seemed only fair. Abuelita had pulled me through the rages of scarlet fever by placing, removing and replacing potato slices on the temples of my forehead; she had seen me through several whippings, an arm broken by a dare-jump off Tío Enrique's toolshed, puberty, and my first lie. Really, I told Amá, it was only fair.

Not that I was her favorite granddaughter or anything special. I wasn't even pretty or nice like my older sisters and I just couldn't do the girl things they could do. My hands were too big to handle the fineries of crocheting or embroidery and I always pricked my fingers or knotted my colored threads time and time again while my sisters laughed and called me bull hands with their cute waterlike voices. So I began keeping a piece of jagged brick in my sock to bash my sisters or anyone who called me bull hands. Once, while we all sat in the bedroom, I hit Teresa on the forehead, right above her eyebrow, and she ran to Amá with her mouth open, her hand over her eye while blood seeped between her fingers. I was used to the whippings by then.

I wasn't respectful either. I even went so far as to doubt the power of Abuelita's slices, the slices she said absorbed my fever. "You're still alive, aren't you?" Abuelita snapped back, her pasty gray eye beaming at me and burning holes in my suspicions. Regretful that I had let secret questions drop out of my mouth, I couldn't look into her eyes. My hands began to fan out, grow like a liar's nose until they hung by my side like low weights. Abuelita made a balm out of dried moth wings and Vicks and rubbed my hands, shaping them back to size. It was the strangest feeling. Like bones melting. Like sun shining through the darkness of your eyelids. I didn't mind helping Abuelita after that, so Amá would always send me over to her.

In the early afternoon Amá would push her hair back,
hand me my sweater and shoes, and tell me to go to Mama
Luna's. This was to avoid another fight and another whip-
ping, I knew. I would deliver one last direct shot on Marisela's
arm and jump out of our house, the slam of the screen door
burying her cries of anger, and I'd gladly go help Abuelita
plant her wild lilies or jasmine or heliotrope or cilantro or
hierbabuena in red Hills Brothers coffee cans. Abuelita would
wait for me at the top step of her porch holding a hammer and
nail and empty coffee cans. And although we hardly spoke,
hardly looked at each other as we worked over root trans-
plants, I always felt her gray eye on me. It made me feel, in a
strange sort of way, safe and guarded and not alone. Like God
was supposed to make you feel.

On Abuelita's porch, I would puncture holes in the bot-
tom of the coffee cans with a nail and a precise hit of a hammer. This completed, my job was to fill them with red clay
mud from beneath her rose bushes, packing it softly, then
making a perfect hole, four fingers round, to nest a sprouting
avocado pit, or the spidery sweet potatoes that Abuelita
rooted in mayonnaise jars with toothpicks and daily water, or
prickly chayotes that produced vines that twisted and wound
all over her porch pillars, crawling to the roof, up and over the
roof, and down the other side, making her small brick house
look like it was cradled within the vines that grew pear-
shaped squashes ready for the pick, ready to be steamed with
onions and cheese and butter. The roots would burst out of
the rusted coffee cans and search for a place to connect. I
would then feed the seedlings with water.

But this was a different kind of help, Amá said, because
Abuelita was dying. Looking into her gray eye, then into her
brown one, the doctor said it was just a matter of days. And so
it seemed only fair that these hands she had melted and
formed found use in rubbing her caving body with alcohol and
marihuana, rubbing her arms and legs, turning her face to
the window so that she could watch the Bird of Paradise
blooming or smell the scent of clove in the air. I toweled her
face frequently and held her hand for hours. Her gray wiry
hair hung over the mattress. Since I could remember, she'd
kept her long hair in braids. Her mouth was vacant and when
she slept, her eyelids never closed all the way. Up close, you
could see her gray eye beaming out the window, staring hard

as if to remember everything. I never kissed her. I left the window open when I went to the market.

Across the street from Jay's Market there was a chapel. I never knew its denomination, but I went in just the same to search for candles. I sat down on one of the pews because there were none. After I cleaned my fingernails, I looked up at the high ceiling. I had forgotten the vastness of these places, the coolness of the marble pillars and the frozen statues with blank eyes. I was alone. I knew why I had never returned.

That was one of Apá's biggest complaints. He would pound his hands on the table, rocking the sugar dish or spilling a cup of coffee and scream that if I didn't go to Mass every Sunday to save my goddamn sinning soul, then I had no reason to go out of the house, period. Punto final. He would grab my arm and dig his nails into me to make sure I understood the importance of catechism. Did he make himself clear? Then he strategically directed his anger at Amá for her lousy ways of bringing up daughters, being disrespectful and unbelieving, and my older sisters would pull me aside and tell me if I didn't get to Mass right this minute, they were all going to kick the holy shit out of me. Why am I so selfish? Can't you see what it's doing to Amá, you idiot? So I would wash my feet and stuff them in my black Easter shoes that shone with Vaseline, grab a missal and veil, and wave good-bye to Amá.

I would walk slowly down Lorena to First to Evergreen, counting the cracks on the cement. On Evergreen I would turn left and walk to Abuelita's. I liked her porch because it was shielded by the vines of the chayotes and I could get a good look at the people and car traffic on Evergreen without them knowing. I would jump up the porch steps, knock on the screen door as I wiped my feet and call Abuelita, mi Abuelita? As I opened the door and stuck my head in, I would catch the gagging scent of toasting chile on the placa. When I entered the sala, she would greet me from the kitchen, wringing her hands in her apron. I'd sit at the corner of the table to keep from being in her way. The chiles made my eyes water. Am I crying? No, Mama Luna, I'm sure not crying. I don't like going to mass, but my eyes watered anyway, the tears dropping on the tablecloth like candle wax. Abuelita lifted the burnt chiles from the fire and sprinkled water on them until the skins began to separate. Placing them in front of me, she turned to check the menudo. I peeled the skins off and put the flimsy, limp-looking green and yellow chiles in the molcajete and began to crush and crush and twist and crush the heart out of the tomato, the clove of garlic, the stupid chiles that made me cry, crushed them until they turned into liquid under my bull hand. With a wooden spoon, I scraped hard to destroy the guilt, and my tears were gone. I put the bowl of chile next to a vase filled with freshly cut roses. Abuelita touched my hand and pointed to the bowl of menudo that steamed in front of me. I spooned some chile into the menudo and rolled a corn tortilla thin with the palms of my hands. As I ate, a fine Sunday breeze entered the kitchen and a rose petal calmly feathered down to the table.

I left the chapel without blessing myself and walked to Jay's. Most of the time Jay didn't have much of anything. The tomatoes were always soft and the cans of Campbell soups had rusted spots on them. There was dust on the tops of cereal boxes. I picked up what I needed: rubbing alcohol, five cans of chicken broth, a big bottle of Pine Sol. At first Jay got mad because I thought I had forgotten the money. But it was there all the time, in my back pocket.

When I returned from the market, I heard Amá crying in Abuelita's kitchen. She looked up at me with puffy eyes. I placed the bags of groceries on the table and began putting the cans of soup away. Amá sobbed quietly. I never kissed her. After a while, I patted her on the back for comfort. Finally: "¿Y mi Amá?" she asked in a whisper, then choked again and cried into her apron.

Abuelita fell off the bed twice yesterday, I said, knowing that I shouldn't have said it and wondering why I wanted to say it because it only made Amá cry harder. I guess I became angry and just so tired of the quarrels and beatings and unanswered prayers and my hands just there hanging helplessly by my side. Amá looked at me again, confused, angry, and her eyes were filled with sorrow. I went outside and sat on the porch swing and watched the people pass. I sat there until she left. I dozed off repeating the words to myself like rosary prayers: when do you stop giving when do you start giving when do you...and when my hands fell from my lap, I awoke to catch them. The sun was setting, an orange glow, and I knew Abuelita was hungry.

There comes a time when the sun is defiant. Just about the time when moods change, inevitable seasons of a day, transitions from one color to another, that hour or minute or second when the sun is finally defeated, finally sinks into the realization that it cannot with all its power to heal or burn, exist forever, there comes an illumination where the sun and earth meet, a final burst of burning red orange fury reminding us that although endings are inevitable, they are necessary for rebirths, and when that time came, just when I switched on the light in the kitchen to open Abuelita's can of soup, it was probably then that she died.

The room smelled of Pine Sol and vomit, and Abuelita had defecated the remains of her cancerous stomach. She had turned to the window and tried to speak, but her mouth remained open and speechless. I heard you, Abuelita, I said, stroking her cheek, I heard you. I opened the windows of the house and let the soup simmer and overboil on the stove. I turned the stove off and poured the soup down the sink. From the cabinet I got a tin basin, filled it with lukewarm water and carried it carefully to the room. I went to the linen closet and took out some modest bleached white towels. With the sacredness of a priest preparing his vestments, I unfolded the towels one by one on my shoulders. I removed the sheets and blankets from her bed and peeled off her thick flannel nightgown. I toweled her puzzled face, stretching out the wrinkles, removing the coils of her neck, toweled her shoulders and breasts. Then I changed the water. I returned to towel the creases of her stretch-marked stomach, her sporadic vaginal hairs, and her sagging thighs. I removed the lint from between her toes and noticed a mapped birthmark on the fold of her buttock. The scars on her back, which were as thin as the life lines on the palms of her hands, made me realize how little I really knew of Abuelita. I covered her with a thin blanket and went into the bathroom. I washed my hands, turned on the tub faucets and watched the water pour into the tub with vitality and steam. When it was full, I turned off the water and undressed. Then I went to get Abuelita.

She was not as heavy as I thought and when I carried her in my arms, her body fell into a V. And yet my legs were tired, shaky, and I felt as if the distance between the bedroom and bathroom was miles and years away. Amá, where are you?

I stepped into the bathtub one leg first, then the other. I bent my knees slowly to descend into the water slowly so I wouldn't scald her skin. There, there, Abuelita, I said, cradling her, smoothing her as we descended, I heard you. Her hair fell back and spread across the water like eagles' wings. The water in the tub overflowed and poured onto the tile of the floor. Then the moths came. Small gray ones that came from her soul and out through her mouth fluttering to light, circling the single dull light bulb of the bathroom. Dying is lonely and I wanted to go to where the moths were, stay with her and plant chayotes whose vines would crawl up her fingers and into the clouds; I wanted to rest my head on her chest with her stroking my hair, telling me about the moths that lay within the soul and slowly eat the spirit up; I wanted to return to the waters of the womb with her so that we would never be alone again. I wanted. I wanted my Amá. I removed a few strands of hair from Abuelita's face and held her small light head within the hollow of my neck. The bathroom was filled with moths, and for the first time in a long time I cried, rocking us, crying for her, for me, for Amá, the sobs emerging from the depths of anguish, the misery of feeling half-born, sobbing until finally the sobs rippled into circles and circles of sadness and relief. There, there, I said to Abuelita, rocking us gently, there, there.

Growing

Growing

The two walked down First Street hand in reluctant hand. The smaller one wore a thick, red sweater which had a desperately loose button that swung like a pendulum. She carried her crayons, humming "Jesus loves little boys and girls" to the speeding echo of the Saturday morning traffic, and was totally oblivious to her older sister's wrath.

"My eye!" Naomi ground out the words from between her teeth. She turned to her youngest sister who seemed unconcerned and quite delighted at the prospect of another adventure. "Chaperone," she said with great disdain. "My EYE!" Lucía was chosen by Apá to be Naomi's chaperone. Infuriated, Naomi dragged her along impatiently, pulling and jerking at almost every step. She was 14, almost 15, the idea of having to be watched by a young snot like Lucía was insulting to her maturity. She flicked her hair over her shoulder. "Goddammit," she murmured, making sure that the words were soft enough so that both God and Lucía could not hear them.

There seemed to be no way out of the custom. Her arguments were always the same and always turned into pleas. This morning was no different. Amá, Naomi said, exasperated but determined not to cower out of this one, Amá, the United States is different. Here girls don't need chaperones. Parents trust their daughters. As usual Amá turned to the kitchen sink or the ice box, shrugged her shoulders and said: "You have to ask your father." Naomi's nostrils flexed in fury as she pleaded. "But, Amá, it's embarrassing. I'm too old for that. I am an adult." And as usual, Apá felt different, and in his house she had absolutely no other choice but to drag Lucía to a sock hop or church carnival or anywhere Apá was sure a social interaction was inevitable. And Lucía came along as a spy, a gnat, a pain in the neck.

Well, Naomi debated with herself, it wasn't Lucía's fault, really. She suddenly felt sympathy for the humming little girl who scrambled to keep up with her as they crossed the freeway overpass. She stopped and tugged Lucía's shorts up, and although her shoelaces were tied, Naomi retied them. No, it wasn't her fault after all, Naomi thought, and she patted her sister's soft light brown almost blondish hair; it was Apá's. She slowed her pace as they continued their journey to Jorge's house. It was Apá who refused to trust her, and she could not understand what she had done to make him so distrustful. *TÚ ERES MUJER*, he thundered like a great voice above the heavens, and that was the end of any argument, any question, because he said those words not as a truth, but as a verdict, and she could almost see the clouds parting, the thunderbolts breaking the tranquility of her sex. Naomi tightened her grasp with the thought, shaking her head in disbelief.

"So what's wrong with being a mujer," she asked herself out loud.

"Wait up. Wait," Lucía said, rushing behind her.

"Well, would you hurry? Would you?" Naomi reconsidered: Lucía did have some fault in the matter after all, and she became irritated at once at Lucía's smile and the way her chaperone had of taking and holding her hand. As they passed El Gallo, Lucía began fussing, hanging on to her older sister's waist for reassurance.

"Stop it. Would you stop it?" She unglued her sister's grasp and continued pulling her along. "What's wrong with you?" she asked Lucía. I'll tell you what's wrong with you, she thought, as they waited at the corner of an intersection for the light to change: You have a big mouth. That's it. If it wasn't for Lucía's willingness to tattle, she would not have been grounded for three months. Three months, twelve Saturday nights and two church bazaars later, Naomi still hadn't forgiven her youngest sister. When they crossed the street, a homely young man with a face full of acne honked at her tight purple pedal pushers. The two were startled by the honk.

"Go to hell," she yelled at the man in the blue and white Chevy. She indignantly continued her walk.

"Don't be mad, my little baby," he said, his car crawling across the street, then speeding off leaving tracks on the pavement. "You make me ache," he yelled, and he was gone.

"GO TO HELL, goddamn you!" she screamed at the top of her lungs, forgetting for a moment that Lucía told everything to Apá. What a big mouth her youngest sister had, for chrissakes. Three months.

Naomi stewed in anger when she thought of the Salesian Carnival and how she first met a Letterman Senior whose eyes, she remembered with a soft smile, sparkled like crystals of brown sugar. She sighed deeply as she recalled the excitement she experienced when she first became aware that he was following them from booth to booth. Joe's hair was greased back and his dimples were deep. When he finally handed her a stuffed rabbit he had won pitching dimes, she knew she wanted him.

As they continued walking, Lucía waved to the Fruit Man. He slipped off his teeth and, again, she was bewildered.

"Would you hurry up!" Naomi told Lucía as she had told her that same night at the carnival. Joe walked beside them and took out a whole roll of tickets, trying to convince her to leave her youngest sister on the ferris wheel. "You could watch her from behind the gym," he had told her, and his eyes smiled pleasure. "Come on," he said, "have a little fun." They waited in the ferris-wheel line of people.

"Stay on the ride," she finally instructed Lucía, making sure her sweater was buttoned. "And when it stops again, just give the man another ticket, okay?" Lucía said okay, excited at the prospect of heights and dips and her stomach wheezing in between. After Naomi saw her go up for the first time, she waved to her, then slipped away into the darkness and joined the other hungry couples behind the gym. Occasionally, she would open her eyes to see the lights of the ferris wheel spinning in the air with dizzy speed.

When Naomi returned to the ferris wheel, her hair undone, her lips still tingling from his newly stubbled cheeks, Lucía walked off and vomited. She vomited the popcorn, a hot dog, some chocolate raisins, and a candied apple. And all Naomi knew was that she was definitely in trouble.

"It was the ferris wheel," Lucía said to Apá. "The wheel going like this over and over again." She circled her arms in the air and vomited again at the thought of it.

"Where was your sister?" Apá had asked, his voice raising.

"I don't know," Lucía replied, and Naomi knew she had just committed a major offense, and Joe would never wait until her prison sentence was completed.

"Owwww," Lucía said. "You're pulling too hard."

"You're a slowpoke, that's why," Naomi snarled back. They crossed the street and passed the rows of junk yards and the shells of cars, which looked like abandoned skull heads. They passed Señora Núñez's neat, wooden house, and Naomi saw her peeking through the curtains of her window. They passed the Tú y Yo, the one-room dirt pit of a liquor store where the men bought their beers and sat outside on the curb drinking quietly. When they reached Fourth Street, Naomi spotted the neighborhood kids playing stickball with a broomstick and a ball. Naomi recognized them right away, and Tina waved to her from the pitcher's mound.

"Wanna play?" Lourdes yelled from center field. "Come on, have some fun."

"Can't," Naomi replied. "I can't." Kids, kids, she thought. My, my. It wasn't more than a few years ago that she played baseball with Eloy and the rest of them. But she was in high school now, too old now, and it was unbecoming of her. She was an adult.

"I'm tired," Lucía said. "I wanna ice cream."

"You got money?"

"No."

"Then shut up." Lucía sat on the curb, hot and tired, and began removing her sweater. Naomi decided to sit down next to her for a few minutes and watch the game. Anyway, she wasn't really that much in a hurry to get to Jorge's. A few minutes wouldn't make much difference to someone who spent most of his time listening to the radio.

She counted them by names. They were all there. Fifteen of them, and their ages varied just as much as their clothes. They dressed in an assortment of colors, and looked like confetti thrown out in the street. Pants, skirts, shorts were always too big and had to be tugged up constantly, and shirt sleeves rolled and unrolled, and socks colorfully mismatched with shoes that did not fit. But the way they dressed presented no obstacle for scoring or yelling foul, and she enjoyed the abandonment with which they played. She knew that the only decision these kids made was what to play next, and for a moment she wished to return to those days.

Chano's team was up. The teams were oddly numbered. Chano had nine on his team because everybody wanted to be on a winning team. It was an unwritten law of stickball that anyone who wanted to play joined in on whatever team they preferred. Tina's team had the family faithful 6. Of course, numbers determined nothing. Naomi remembered once playing with Eloy and three of her cousins against ten players, and still winning by three points.

Chano was at bat and everybody fanned out far and wide. He was a power hitter and Tina's team prepared for him. They could not afford a home run now because Piri was on second, legs apart, waiting to rush home and score. And Piri wanted to score at all costs. It was important for him because his father sat watching the game outside the liquor store with a couple of his uncles and a couple of malt liquors.

"Steal the base," his father yelled. "Run, menso." But Piri hesitated. He was too afraid to take the risk. Tina pitched and Chano swung, missed, strike one.

"Batter, batter, swing," Naomi yelled from the curb. She stood to watch the action better.

"I wanna ice cream," Lucía said.

"Come on, Chano," Piri yelled, bending his knees and resting his hands on them like a true baseball player. He spat, clapped his hands. "Come on."

"Ah, shut up, sissy." This came from Lourdes, Tina's younger sister. Naomi smiled at the rivals. "Can't you see you're making the pitcher nervous?" She pushed him hard between the shoulder blades, then returned to her position in the outfield, holding her hand over her eyes to shield them from the sun. "Strike the batter out," she screamed at the top of her lungs. "Come on, strike the menso out!" Tina delivered another pitch, but not before going through the motions of a professional preparing for the perfect pitch. Naomi knew she was a much better pitcher than Tina. Strike two. Maybe not. Lourdes let out such a cry of joy that Piri's father called her a dog.

Chano was angry now, nervous and upset. He put his bat down, spat in his hands and rubbed them together, wiped the sides of his jeans, kicked the dirt for perfect footing.

"Get on with the game," Naomi shouted impatiently. Chano tested his swing. He swung so hard that he caused Juan, Tina's brother and devoted catcher, to jump back.

"Hey, baboso, watch out," Juan said. "You almost hit my coco." And he pointed to his forehead.

"Well, don't be so stupid," Chano replied, positioning himself once again. "Next time, back off when I come to bat."

"Baboso," Juan repeated.

"Say it to my face," Chano said, breaking his stance and turning to Juan. Say it again so I can break this bat over your head."

"Ah, come on," Kiki, the shortstop, yelled. "I gotta go home pretty soon."

"Let up," Tina demanded.

"Shut up, marrana," Piri said, turning to his father to make sure he heard. "Tinasana, cola de marrana. Tinasana, cola de marrana." Tina became so infuriated that she threw the ball directly at his stomach. Piri folded over in pain.

"No! No!" Sylvia yelled. "Don't get off the base or she'll tag you out."

"It's a trick," Miguel yelled from behind home plate.

"That's what you get!" This came from Lourdes. Piri did not move, and although Naomi felt sorry for him, she giggled at the scene just the same.

"I heard the ice-cream man," Lucía said.

"You're all right, Tina," Naomi yelled, laughing. "You're A-O-K." And with that compliment, Tina took a bow for her performance until everyone began shouting and booing. Tina was prepared. She pitched and Chano made the connection quick, hard, the ball rising high and flying over Piri's, Lourdes', Naomi's and Lucía's heads and landing inside the Chinese Cemetery.

"DON'T JUST STAND THERE!!" Tina screamed to Lourdes. "Go get it, stupid." After Lourdes broke out of her trance, she ran to the tall chain-link fence which surrounded the cemetery, jumped on it with great urgency and crawled up like a scrambling spider. When she jumped over the top of the fence, her dress tore with a rip-roar.

"We saw your calzones, we saw your calzones," Lucía sang.

"Go! Lourdes, go!" Naomi jumped up and down in excitement, feeling like a player who so much wanted to help her team win, but was benched on the sidelines for good. The kids blended into one huge noise, like an untuned orchestra, screaming and shouting, Get the Ball, Run in, Piri, Go Lourdes, Go, Throw the ball, Chano pick up your feetthrowtheballrunrunrunthrow the ball. *THROW* the ball to me!!" Naomi waved and waved her arms. She was no longer concerned with her age, her menstruations, her breasts that bounced with every jump. All she wanted was an out at home plate. To hell with being benched. "Throw it to me," she yelled.

In the meantime, Lourdes searched frantically for the ball, tip-toeing across the graves saying, excuse me, please excuse me, excuse me, until she found the ball peacefully buried behind a huge gray marble stone, and she yelled to no one in particular, CATCH IT, SOMEONE CATCH IT. She threw the ball up and over the fence and it landed near Lucía. Lucía was about to reach for it when Naomi picked it off the ground and threw it straight to Tina. Tina caught the ball, dropped it, picked it up, and was about to throw it to Juan at home plate when she realized that Juan had picked up home plate and run, zig-zagging across the street while Piri and Chano ran after him. Chano was a much faster runner, but Piri insisted that he be the first to touch the base.

"I gotta touch it first," he kept repeating between pants. "I gotta." The kids on both teams grew wild with anger and encouragement. Seeing an opportunity, Tina ran as fast as her stocky legs could take her. Because Chano slowed down to let Piri touch the base first, Tina was able to reach him, and with one quick blow, she thundered OUT! She made one last desperate throw to Juan so that he could tag Piri out, but she threw it so hard that it struck Piri right in the back of his head, and the blow forced him to stumble just within reach of Juan and home plate.

"You're out!!" Tina said, out of breath. "O-U-T, out."

"No fair!" Piri immediately screamed. "NO FAIR!!" He stomped his feet in rage. "You marrana, you marrana."

"Don't be such a baby. Take it like a man," Piri's father said as he opened another malt liquor with a can opener. But Piri continued stomping and screaming until his shouts were buried by the honk of an oncoming car and the kids obediently opened up like a zipper to let the car pass.

Naomi felt like a victor. She had helped once again. Delighted, she giggled, laughed, laughed harder, suppressed her laughter into chuckles, then laughed again. Lucía sat quietly, to her surprise, and her eyes were heavy with sleep. She wiped them, looked at Naomi. "Vamos," Naomi said, offering her hand. By the end of the block, she lifted Lucía and laid her head on her shoulder. As Lucía fell asleep, Naomi won-

dered why things were always so complicated once you
became older. Funny how the old want to be young and the
young want to be old. She was guilty of that. Now that she
was older, her obligations became heavier both at home and
at school. There were too many expectations, and no one
instructed her on how to fulfill them, and wasn't it crazy? She
cradled Lucía gently, kissed her cheek. They were almost at
Jorge's now, and reading to him was just one more thing she
dreaded, and one more thing she had no control over: it was
another one of Apá's thunderous commands.

When she was Lucía's age, she hunted for lizards and
played stickball with her cousins. When her body began to
bleed at twelve, Eloy saw her in a different light. Under the
house, he sucked her swelling nipples and became jealous
when she spoke to other boys. He no longer wanted to throw
rocks at the cars on the freeway with her and she began to act
differently because everyone began treating her differently
and wasn't it crazy? She could no longer be herself, and her
father could no longer trust her because she was a woman.
Jorge's gate hung on a hinge and she was almost afraid it
would fall off when she opened it. She felt Lucía's warm, deep
breath on her neck and it tickled her.

"Tomorrow," she whispered lovingly to her sister as she
entered the yard. "Tomorrow I'll buy you all the ice creams
you want."

Birthday

Birthday

(At the moment, there are only two things I am sure of: my name is Alice and all I want to do is sleep. I want to sleep so badly that I am angry at their conspiracy to keep me awake. Why so early? I want to knot myself into a little ball and sleep. I will knot myself into a little ball and sleep. I will. I will become you, knotted stomach.)

> *finally bonded drifting afloat i become, and how much i love it. craft cradles me drifting far. far away. the waves rock me into an anxious sleepless sleep, and i love it—God, how much i love it. brimming baptism roll. swell. thunder. reaching up to vastness. calm. i relax beneath the fluids that thicken like jelly. Thickening. i am transparent and light, ounceless. spinning with each breath you exhale. i move closer and closer to the shore and i love it.*

I rub my stomach because it aches. (Would I like to stay Alice, or become a mama?) I rub my stomach again as I sit on the couch (perhaps unconsciously hoping the rubbing will unknot my...my baby? No, doesn't sound right. Baby-to-be? Isn't the same. Isn't.) I sit, my arms folded, on a vinyl plastic couch which squeaks every time I cross or recross my legs. One of my legs swings back and forth. My breath is misty and I exhale hard to watch it form into smoke. Unfolding my arms, I lift my hands to my face and my fingers massage my eyelids. Blurred. Slowly focusing the room. A living room converted into a waiting room. Across from me a small fireplace. An off-white wall supports a single picture of snow and church. Dusty. Everything is dusty. In an isolated corner, a wire chair stands. Big room; practically empty. One dirty window pasted with announcements.

"I don't know *why*, that's all." And that was all it had come to. "Now will you please stop bugging me?" Her voice became thorny with these last words, and she was now more annoyed than hurt. How many times had she asked herself that same question which became implanted in her mind and soon germinated into a monstrous sponge, leaving no room for an answer?

He finally lifted his eyes off the lawn and shifted his glance to her face. Slowly, he continued, "It's the twentieth century..." Again he shook his head in disbelief and his eyes glanced over her shoulder and into nothing. "Why weren't you taking anything? You know better..." He paused, wet his lips and sighed. "You're a girl. You're supposed to know those things."

"Don't. Don't. I don't know why." She felt sorry for him and her voice became increasingly soft. "What do you think we ought to do?" He looked down at the blotches of dirt and grass, staring hard, as if the answer laid beneath.

"You'll have to get an abort..."

"Wait." She couldn't breathe and she held her hand to his lips so that the word would not be mentioned out loud and therefore made a real possibility. "Let's...we gotta think this over." There was a long pause between them. The wind blew weak leaves off the tree they sat under, and, she thought, weak leaves enjoy the moment of freedom faster, but they die sooner. She realized now, suffering from this heaviness on her heart, that the decision was ultimately hers and hers alone. Her eyes, that had first pleaded desperately under the tree, now looked upon him as a frightened child.

"Alice." She turned to him and a reassuring smile appeared on her face. She hugged him tenderly and whispered, "You're just making it worse for both of us." Hers. The wind blew a colder breeze and they comforted themselves with an embrace.

A girl with long stringy hair enters the room followed by a chilly draft that slaps me on the back (I hope I don't look *that* bad). She sits on the lonely wire chair. I smile at her with lazy lips, but the encouraging gesture is not returned. (Oily hair. Looks like she used mayonnaise for shampoo.) I belch out a giggle. (Alice—now's not the time to joke.) I keep swinging my legs until my heart swells and I choke—Oh my God...

My God, what am I doing here? Alone and cold. And afraid. Damn, dammit. I should have stayed a virgin. STUPID, stupid! Virgins have babies, too. Enough Alice. Keep warm, Alice. No sex, Alice. Punishing me. For loving, God? Fucking, Alice. Fucking Alice. Stop it, Alice. Alice. Grow up, not out.

Alice.

God isn't pregnant.

Alice.

"Alice. Alice Johnson."

"Me." I nod my head and smile. I think I'm going to win.

"Then *you* must be Cynthia Simmons." The girl with the mayonnaise hair barely nods her head. "It sure is cold in here..." I smile in agreement. I don't feel like small talk. "My name is Kathy." She resembles a small elf. A petite and skinny girl wearing an orange dress and white tights that gather at her bony knees. "...Follow me, please..." We follow her like zombies into another larger room. On one side, test tubes, desk lights, bottles; on the other, desks and telephones. The room was probably a kitchen before. Cabinets, like Terry's kitchen.

"How do I realize these things? Y'know the feeling. I was a whole invisible. I felt so light, I automatically took everything lightly. The responsibility of having a child didn't fit into my scheme of loving. To me, to me, Terry..." She paused to take another sip of jasmine tea. The light of the kitchen made a round, bright ring on the table where Alice put her cup down. "...love was satisfaction, happiness, and all that other bullshit, not babies." Terry gestured mocking amazement with a dull smirk which impelled Alice to defend herself. "Babies, yea, sure, but not in the real sense. Not me."

Terry sat across from her and munched on graham crackers throughout the evening. Alice searched for some evidence of sympathetic understanding from her, but all Terry seemed to do was munch slowly on a cracker, once in a while dipping it into her tea.

"Relax, Alice. My God, you would think it was the end of the world." She said it with such an air of nonchalance that

Alice became angry, and yet comforted by her words. (Tell me what to do.) "How does Mike feel about it?"

"I haven't really told him...I mean, nothing definite. This is all so unreal." She tried to hide the tears from Terry. A moment later Terry stood up from the table. Alice's eyes followed her to the living room. She picked up her phone book and, with the slowness of thick molasses, returned to her chair. She opened the book. "Here, take this number down..."

"What's this? Dial-A-Prayer?" Neither of them laughed. Alice copied the number down, hesitating to ask her what place it belonged to, but nonetheless trusting Terry's experience and age. She thought of Terry as an experienced woman at twenty-one. She was a big-boned female with high cheekbones that did not give her face away to any genre of feeling. Yet, Terry was sensuously beautiful. She was her own best friend and took responsibility for her actions. Her coolness in the hottest situations always troubled Alice. She knew Terry concealed all her emotions behind a facade, an almost perfect unbreakable mask, and she hoped to see the day her flowing warmth would turn into blazes unchecked.

Terry was Alice's best friend.

"It's to the Woman's Abortion Referral Center, in case..." and that was all it had come to.

"Why are you so sure I want an abortion?"

"You don't?"

"I just haven't made up my mind yet." Terry picked up a cracker and munched on it. Alice knew what was coming.

"We both know you can't have a child. You're young and dreamy. That won't help you or your child any. Look, you'll stew and brood and feel pitiful and pray until your knees chap, but in the end, you'll decide on the abortion. So why not cut out all this silliness."

"I wish it were all that easy. But you wouldn't know how it feels. I wish it were..." Alice couldn't finish the sentence. Instead she watched Terry's silent flowing stream of mascara crack the cheeks of her face. She reached down to get Alice's hand and patted it gently.

"I do know, Alice."

(Terry, I hear your voice floating on and on and on. It was my decision that seemed already decided for me. I don't have to go through it. But here I am now, bringing out the money to pay. Lack of sleep, so early. That's why I don't feel good.)

"...and here is your receipt. Now that we have the business over with, I want you girls to fill out these forms..." I make neat "X's" in the boxes next to the word "no." The girl sitting next to me begins to redden and her eyes melt. I don't know what to do so I smile and she returns it. Kathy enters again with some lemonade and wheat crackers. (Good, all I had this morning was a hershey bar.)

I sit on the toilet seat with a paper cup under me. Damn cold, and early. At last. (AH! The trickling of today's morning water.) The warmth of my urine makes my stomach turn. As I walk out with my warm paper cup, I glance at the waiting room. There are many girls now sitting and waiting.

The lid of the university opens up. Watercolored people slowly emerge, moving endlessly about the thick cemented walls. I want so much to disappear. I sit under the tree with my pile of books and look at the quiet people; they float like balloons. I hope everything will be better when he comes. Arrived as expected. No kiss, a simple smile. Sits next to me. For a moment, I feel resentment towards him. We begin a conversation and I feel myself replying but instantly forgetting what I say or hear. Sometimes I feel myself giggling at his remarks, while other times my head automatically nods in agreement to whatever he says. Then by the expression on his face, by the pounding of his heart that buries all other sounds, by the watercolors fusing into nothing, I realize I've told him I am pregnant.

"I don't know *why*, that's all." And that was all it had come to. "Alice."

Alice

"Alice. Alice Johnson."

"Me."

"My, that *is* a pretty dress. The name's Sharon and I'll be assisting the doctor in the procedure." I smile. I follow her into a small doctor's office. Clean and white with silver objects that reflect my face in distortion. (Oh, God, my God, forgive me for I have sinned.)

"Shall I take off my dress?" "No, no need to." I remove my clean underwear and place my feet on the stirrups with great caution. The thick paper under me crinkles. It is so cold.

Kathy enters the room while Sharon prepares the vacuum-like machine.

"Would you like me to stay with you? You *are* the first of the morning, y'know. (I know) I nod. She's a nice girl. She pulls my dress up a little more and removes my slip. Sharon is moving a utility table near the stirrups as the little elf begins to rub my thighs. The doctor enters the room. Cold. Her hands are very cold. "Relax. Think of something that you love." Kathy continues rubbing my thighs. "Relax," Sharon reasures me. "Relax," the doctor demands.

"Tell me, Alice, so what are you taking up in school... *finally bonded drifting afloat i become, and how much i love it. Cold hands. Forgive me, Father, for I have...* Music. How nice! Are you into Classical or...*craft cradles me drifting farther away; and how much i love it.* The operation takes about 5 minutes. Now the doctor will insert...*the waves rock me into an anxious sleepless sleep. And i love. No! I don't love you, not you, God, knotted ball. I hate you, Alice.* What other instruments do you play? *brimming baptism waters roll. swell. thunder.* Relax, Alice, and try not to move again. *reaching up to the vastness. calm. i relax under the fluids that thicken like jelly.* i am still; my body is transparent and light, ounceless.

The Broken Web

The Broken Web

I

His quick-paced footsteps sounded throughout the hollowness of the church and grew louder as he approached the pew where she sat, cold and chaste as the stone shapes of the holy family. Her eyes had followed the silent figure of a shriveled woman performing the ritual of candlelighting before her ears became aware of his footsteps. The black-robed priest passed her, and soon the footsteps dissolved into the distance. He disappeared inside the dark vacuum of the confessional booth.

He entered the middle booth and waited for the first sign of early morning's sinners. The door to his left opened and closed. Leaning his ear near the small black-screened window, the priest waited until he heard the protesting creak the leather made when the heaviness of the sinner's knee rested against it before opening its panes.

"Bless me, Father, for I have sinned. It has been four days since..."

It was always the same monotonous whisper; man and girl and boy and woman—no real difference. They came to him seeking redemption; they had stepped into the realm of sin; they had all slapped his walls with hideous, ridiculously funny and often imaginary sins—and they all expected him to erase their sins, to ease their souls so that they could, with the innocence of a pure heart, enter into sin once again. The whispering tune of secrets hidden and finally banished.

"The dream, Father, I am still having that bad dream."

"Are you dreaming unnatural acts?" He drummed his fingers on his knees.

"I think so. At least it is to me, Father."

"Is it anything sexual?"

"No." He wasn't listening, was he? "No," she repeated. "It's like a nightmare. I close my eyes and there is darkness. I think I'm asleep, then..."

He heard movement.

"...then, my eyelids become one black screen. I anticipate a movie or something. While I am waiting, I begin to hear voices. It's my father, talking loud, his words loud and slurred. They're arguing about something. Something having to do with my mother, then...No. Something having to do with my father. I still see the screen before my eyes, but I'm so sleepy. Yreina, you know her, Father, my younger sister, begs me to pray to God to make the voices stop. But you see, Father, I can't because I'm asleep, and when you're asleep, you don't know what's going on. Everything is not real, and so the voices aren't real and I wanted it that way. By morning, I would open my eyes with no memory, nothing. So I wasn't supposed to know what was happening."

She stopped there, and again he heard movement.

"Go on," he heard himself say.

"I'm asleep; I see a speck on the screen. A faraway speck coming closer and bigger and bigger and closer and soon the speck shapes into a statue. Our Lord with His hands outstretched. I feel comforted, even if He is only a statue in the living room. I don't hear voices. Good. I'm asleep."

Again there was silence. He hadn't had breakfast yet and his stomach gurgled in anger. She continued.

"There He stands. Solid. But what happened next I will never understand. I will never be able to forgive myself for letting it happen. I heard something, something loud. A bullet sound. It rang. The ringing visualized into a tail connected to the bullet sound. I saw it pierce the image, burst like a firecracker. Sparks. Pierce it into little pieces before my eyes, flashing light on the screen. I think I know what happened, but it's a dream. I'm asleep, you see."

He's on the couch. Please, my God, he's full of blood. Wake up, Martha, quick, pleaseohmygod...Someone broke a statue of Jesus—the one with His hands outstretched, and now he's bleeding on the couch. I heard the crash and the bones shatter like sparks from wall to wall, but I want to be left alone. *He's bleeding all over the*...I keep my eyelids cemented together and I wish I could stuff rags in her volcanic mouth.

But Yreina's an eruption. I heard the explosion, goddammit, so leave me alone. I was sinking into the mattress until I could barely see the tops of my warm sheets. Then, with the burst, I was vomiting on top of them. Stay asleep. So good to sleep. I act as if Yreina is just another addition to my sleep. I feel hands, cold and tight around my neck as Yreina screams *Wake up, Martha, jesusmío, Mama shot...*

II

The saloon consisted of various kitchen tables and chairs colored from egg-yolk yellows to checkered red and whites. Although it was the rainy mid-March season, deflated balloons and faded crepe paper remained on the ceiling as a reminder of a never-ceasing New Year celebration. Christmas lights shone against two mirrors on one wall directly behind the bar. The dance floor was a small area made up of cracked, unsettled tiles often caked with mud until Olivia cleaned them early the next morning. Olivia, the evening barmaid and morning cleaning woman of Los Amigos, mopped the floors with a thick heavy cloth connected to a mop stick. Her shoulders tired of pushpulling the mop; the ache soon dropped from her shoulders and concentrated in her legs and feet—those same dancing feet that patted the mud tighter into the cracks of the tiles.

It was the rainy season and business seemed slower than usual, for although there was still an even flow of customers, the tips dwindled to almost nothing. This time, however, Olivia didn't mind all that much; she looked forward to seeing the man who had, without knowing it, unburied her feelings of loneliness and at the same time given her anticipated pleasure by just being in the same room with her. Presently, he was the man she secretly loved.

She had not felt like this in a very long time; moonwarm and tender for another person. She loved once before, but not secretly. She lived openly with him, bringing forth two sons. And what a scandal that had caused! If she would have to live an outcast, she would do so for him. But he left one afternoon. The room was getting hotter.

Oh, but could he love. Love her anywhere, anyplace. She remembered when she thought her head had exploded and bled between her legs when he first made love to her on the roof of her house. She could remember that slow-slap, faint-slap, almost monotonous-slap of her mother making tortillas in the kitchen right beneath them turn into an intense applause...and then she hated him, his two sons—thank goodness she gave them her name—and finally love itself. Her arms thrust the mopstick harder.

But Tomás. He was not a coward. Someday, she would have to let him know how she felt. But she couldn't, shouldn't wait too long. Already her youth was peeling off her face like the paint on the saloon walls. Olivia stopped to inspect the job. The dance floor was ready for tonight.

Olivia thought of her two sons as she locked the front doors of the saloon, proud of herself for being the only other person to hold the key to the establishment, and she smiled that smile when she remembered the roof incident. The key; just her and the old man. The old, tight, stinky sonofabitch, she thought. It was noon and the streets of Tijuana were flooded with puddles of muddy water. Two kids bathed near the street corner and the Saturday tourists waved like national flags along the sidewalks. The air was unusually fresh and she looked up at the sky. It will be a good night tonight, she thought as she hurried home.

Tomás's wife was a statue-tall woman with floods of thick black hair that reached to the folds of her buttocks. She watched her reflection in the mirror, brushing her hair with slow moving strokes. She enjoyed the luxury of time and the full view of herself. It was like a vacation long deserved, to stay at a place where she didn't have to make beds or clean toilets, or wash off graphic depictions of sexual acts penciled on the walls. Although he did not bring her on his trips across the border to Tijuana (using the excuse that it would be dangerous for her since she would probably be jailed along with him if he were ever caught passing *mexicanos* without proper papers), he asked her to come as far as Chula Vista. Perhaps he thought she needed the rest from her duties as wife and mother, and only in complete solitude did she feel like a woman. Too soon would the grape harvest return; the Fresno sun was almost mockingly waiting to bleed the sweat from all five of them. All five. *Mis niños.* Next time she would bring Martha, Yreina and Miguelito. She braided her hair. He had gone attending business in Tijuana and would not be back for two hours. He would pick her up later and they would go to the saloon tonight. Tomás' wife wondered if that old barmaid (what-was-her-name-now?) still worked there and she wondered if Tomás left her, would she become like her? Weary of travel, she rested her body on the fresh-sheeted soft bed.

Olivia had always avoided looking at herself completely in the mirror; her eyes focused only on the part she attended to. She knew age was nesting. The short skirt revealed her skinny legs that knotted at the knees, and her small but protruding belly surpassed her breasts. Yet she tried making the best of it. With a low-cut blouse and wearing her hair down, she would not be called a vieja so often. Like an artist, she began creating her illusionary eyes with the colors of a forest.

Tomás's wife dreamt of houses. Big ones that would belong to all five of them. A color T.V. and an island. She dreamt of her mother, dozens of diapers blazing, and an invisible bird with huge wings.

Two large false lashes were glued expertly on her natural ones. The eyes were traced with liner and the eyelids finely painted with eye shadow. Done. She lit a cigarette and sat in front of the mirror, re-evaluating the masterpiece. Now, not even the make-up covered her deeper wrinkles. Olivia put her cigarette down, wet her fingers with her tongue, and rubbed away the chappedness of her elbows.

Tomás's wife stretched out slowly, awakening like a cat. It was later than she had anticipated; she hurried to unbraid her hair and continued brushing it as he entered the room, carrying a bag of sweet bread, two bright pink and green ponchos wrapped in transparent paper, and a toy rifle, resembling his own, for Miguelito.
"For the niños." He laid the purchases on the bed. "Tomorrow we have to leave early. I'll have to return next week." Only then will the gente be ready and waiting at Los Amigos." To Tomás' wife this meant that he would not take her across the border and into Tijuana. She understood him well, although he said nothing; her vacation was cut short. Tomás unbuttoned his shirt, pulled off his dusty shoes, and went into the bathroom. There was a flushing sound of the toilet, then the rush of water in the shower. She put her hair

up in a bun, disrobed, and entered the shower with him discreetly.

The perfume was the final touch. Olivia left some tacos and three dollars on the kitchen table. She never knew exactly when her sons came home nor when she herself would, so she left food and money always. It was a silent contract that they had with one another; she never played mother and they, in turn, never asked her to. Olivia blessed herself, sighed, and hurried to the saloon anticipating Tomás' laugh.

III

The promise of night disappeared. He would probably awaken disoriented and bewildered at the unfamiliar room, she thought. But she would assure him that nothing happened because nothing did happen. Tomás had sunk onto the cracked dance-floor tile after that last shot of José Cuervo, drunk, and she had asked his companions to take him to her place. Tomorrow he was leaving for Fresno, to go to his wife, and who knows when she would see him again. Tomás— buried beneath the blankness that liquor caused—slept soundly, unyielding to the fingers that petted and comforted him.

Olivia undressed and lay close to him, defeated but warm. The heaviness of his slow breathing and his oppressive presence held blocks against her sleep. She rested her hand against the firm folds of his breasts, crushing his unraveled curls. Her hand caught the rhythm of his breath. She heard the Sunday morning church bells summon the mourning, sleepless women with dust on their hair, and she would have to wake him before the dawn revealed her secret. Today he was returning to Fresno.

"Tomás." She hoped to awaken him, but all he did was grunt and jerk away from her. The bells of the church rang heavy in the air. Olivia touched his shoulder.

"Tomás." The bells faded. "Sometimes in my sleep," she whispered to him as if speaking to a child not yet born of its senses, "...I can see the inside of me. Mesh. It looks like mesh. Pieces of bones rattling like ice in an empty glass. Those are times I wish I was an artist so I could paint a picture of myself..." Olivia closed her eyes. "...Lime-light green, dull yellow, mixed together like vomit." She turned away from him, facing the window. The cool awakening gray-glow dawn illuminated the room slowly.

"It's true, Tomás. It's true," she whispered to the window. "Sometimes in your sleep, you can see the inside of you." His snoring was like the soft hum of a bee next to her ears. She became still, almost tranquil as that morning, and her eyes bled tears, first quiet flowing tears, then hot, salty stabbing tears uncontrolled, while his snoring was like the soft hum of a bee next to her ears.

IV

"What are you raving about? You think you're not guilty? You, a whore, a bitch! I'm not finished, stay. Before I hit you again. And again. But you won't cry in front of me, will you? You won't please me by unveiling your pain, will you? Let them hear. They're probably not mine anyway.

"The marihuana opiates, the liquor seduces. That is why nothing can hurt me, not even you. I work to live, and I hate it. I live for you, and I hate it. I have another shot of tequila—tequila is a good mistress—and two more before I ask myself, why live?

"I loved you too much. Now I have no pride, no respect for myself. I'm waiting for the breeze that will lift and carry me away from you.

"Ha. Ha. You say that I am unfaithful? In Tijuana, last week? Like the devil, you disguise yourself as a gnat to spy on me? I should have spied on you that night you let him rip the virginity out of you, the blood and slime of your innocence trailing down the sides of his mouth. You tramp. You righteous bitch. Don't I have the right to be unfaithful? Weren't you? Vete mucho a chingar a tu madre, más cabrona que la chingada..."

Martha, please pray to God to make them stop. God doesn't listen to me.

"Perra, don't rage to me about that barmaid! Answer me, vieja cabrona, ans..."

Like a drowning, hissing fire, his ghost smoldered while he lay there. Tomás' wife thought of towers crumbling and then of his intoxicants that unleash and loosen those hidden

passions that burn through the soul and float up to a smolder-
ing belch, causing him to rage that pure rage that no one
really knew of. Tomás was now an invincible cloud of the
past, she thought. A coiled smoking ghost. She kneeled beside
him, laying her puzzle-piece heart against his unliving one.
Unliving because she had pressured the trigger tight, then
tightfingered it until his chest blew up, spilling the oozing
blood that stained all tomorrows. And yet he seemed more
alive. No. More real than anything, anyone around her. She
spoke to him with the voice of prayer. "And you? The choice
was yours, Tomás. As for me, I had no choice. I had given up
being a woman for you, just like you gave up your own respect
and dignity when you married me. Surely now, at this
moment, I feel so close to you; equally dead, but equally real."
How could she explain to him that she was so tired and wrinkled and torn by him, his God, and his word? She had tried to
defy the rules by sleeping with another man, but that only
left her worse off. And she could not leave him because she no
longer owned herself. He owned her, her children owned her,
and she needed them all to live. And she was tired of needing.

What to tell the police, what to say. Tomás's unfaithful-
ness. That was as real as his body on the couch. "Tomás was a
trustful man, but flesh is flesh, men are men..."

The acid fumes that fiercely clawed her insides crept
timidly away from her and mingled with the roaming urinal
scent of the hospital cell. Her children in time would forgive
her. But God? He would never understand; He was a man,
too. No. She would become a cricket wailing nightly for
redemption. That suited her; she would be wailing for
redemption. With the strength of defiant resignation, she
stared zombie-like at the name printed on the wristband.

V

"She moaned a lot in her sleep and sometimes she'd say
things out loud that she'd never say awake. Since we slept in
the same bed, she would sometimes hang onto me and call me
by his name. It wasn't your father's name though; it wasn't
Tomás.

"Under other circumstances, if you had asked me these
questions, I would have belted you hard, as I often did to curi-
ous children who peeked through my window. I am old now,

old and with the same name, and I tell you these things
because soon you will be ready for marriage and the worms
will cover me completely and it'll be too late to tell you anything. How uncomfortable, these worms; today I found two of
them squirming around my toes. Yesterday I found one bur-
rowing into my thigh. I kill them, but I am losing my
strength.

"I am not an evil woman, Martha, but my body has suf-
fered much. Look at this body—twisted like tangled tree
roots. Hand me that glass of water, Martita, I am dry. A little
warm, but good. So you want to know about your parents?
Damn fly. Flies drop dead all around this house. Just the
other day, one fell into my teeth glass. For God's life, I could-
n't bring myself to put on my teeth. Wretched things, these
teeth.

"As you know, I am your oldest aunt. Because I was the
first, our mother—not knowing how many daughters she
would have—saved the beauty that was supposed to be
shared among us. Since I was the first-born daughter, she
gave me bad teeth, and since your mother was the last, she
gave her all the beauty she denied her other daughters,
including me. I remember an old boyfriend of mine. Alejan-
dro? No, Alfredo. Alfredo was his name. He used to tell me,
'Smile, chica, smile, so I can see my reflection.' He was a good
man, that Alfredo. You know, Martha, Alfredo and I were
going to get married once. I knew him for years and years and
he always called me Little Rabbit because of my teeth. But
once he began to notice your mother's developing breasts, and
I caught her giving him that look, I told him to go far away.
He was a good man, that Alfredo.

"It is already getting dark. Please light Jesucristo's candle for me. The days seem so short now. You will say a rosary
with me before you go, won't you? What did you say? What
was your father doing all this time? Tempting the dreams of
older women, that Tomás. I had my eye out for him long
before his voice even changed. But your mother gave him the
look, and I had no right to tell him to go away. From the very
beginning, he gave himself completely to her. And that was a
mistake. Because her heart was just a seed then, she could
not give him something she had not yet created. This drove
Tomás crazy and I would tell her, tell her, 'It is evil to make
him suffer,' and your mother would say, 'I can't help it if he

loves me.' He asked me to watch over your mother, that Tomás.

"Jesús mío, but it gets cold in here. My body begins to freeze at the feet and by morning I am a snow cone. Thank you for the blanket, Martita. Now where was...oh. Many weeks pass. One late night—did I tell you that we shared a bed, your mother and I? Well, one late night I hear tapping on the window. I think it's Tomás coming to get her and I act as if nothing awakes me. Your mother slips out from between the sheets like a snake shedding its skin. She opens the window and they exchange whispers. It is a man all right, but not Tomás.

"God have mercy on my soul, child, but you are a good Martita who must know the truth or else you'll never be at peace and this is why I hope I am not wrong in telling you.

"The man waited outside while your mother felt around the dark room for her robe. I burst out in loud whispers asking her where she is going and who is that man. 'I'll return,' is all she answers. After a long while I am awakened by a cold weight smelling of soft dirt and grass. It was her, breathing as if she had run for miles. Tomás returned about three months after, and I, though years paint coats of vagueness on memories, will never forget the look on Tomás' face when your mother greeted him on the porch with a small belly. They got married a few days later.

"Do you hear the crickets? Our mother warned us against killing crickets because they are the souls of condemned people. Do you hear their wailing, Martita? They conduct the mass of the dead only at night. You will say a rosary with me tonight, won't you?"

The Cariboo Cafe

The Cariboo Cafe

I

They arrived in the secrecy of night, as displaced people often do, stopping over for a week, a month, eventually staying a lifetime. The plan was simple. Mother would work, too, until they saved enough to move into a finer future where the toilet was one's own and the children needn't be frightened. In the meantime, they played in the back alleys, among the broken glass, wise to the ways of the streets. Rule one: never talk to strangers, not even the neighbor who paced up and down the hallways talking to himself. Rule two: the police, or "polie" as Sonya's popi pronounced the word, was La Migra in disguise and thus should always be avoided. Rule three: keep your key with you at all times—the four walls of the apartment were the only protection against the streets until Popi returned home.

Sonya considered her key a guardian saint and she wore it around her neck as such until this afternoon. Gone was the string with the big knot. Gone was the key. She hadn't noticed its disappearance until she picked up Macky from Mrs. Avila's house and walked home. She remembered playing with it as Amá walked her to school. But lunch break came, and Lalo wrestled her down so that he could see her underwear, and it probably fell somewhere between the iron rings and sandbox. Sitting on the front steps of the apartment building, she considered how to explain the missing key without having to reveal what Lalo had seen, for she wasn't quite sure which offense carried the worse penalty.

She watched people piling in and spilling out of the buses, watched an old man asleep on the bus bench across the street. He resembled a crumbled ball of paper, huddled up in the security of a tattered coat. She became aware of their mutual loneliness and she rested her head against her knees, blackened by the soot of the playground asphalt.

The old man eventually awoke, yawned like a lion's roar, unfolded his limbs and staggered to the alley where he urinated between two trash bins. (She wanted to peek, but it was Macky who turned to look.) He zipped up, drank from a paper bag, and she watched him until he disappeared around the corner. As time passed, buses came less frequently, and every other person seemed to resemble Popi. Macky became bored. He picked through the trash barrel; later, and to Sonya's fright, he ran into the street after a pigeon. She understood his restlessness, for waiting was as relentless as long lines to the bathroom. When a small boy walked by, licking away at a scoop of vanilla ice cream, Macky ran after him. In his haste to outrun Sonya's grasp, he fell and tore the knee of his denim jeans. He began to cry, wiping snot against his sweater sleeve.

"See?" she asked, dragging him back to the porch steps by his wrist. "See? God punished you!" It was a thing she always said because it seemed to work. Terrified by the scrawny tortured man on the cross, Macky wanted to avoid His wrath as much as possible. She sat him on the steps in one gruff jerk. Seeing his torn jeans and her own scraped knees, she wanted to join in his sorrow and cry. Instead, she snuggled so close to him she could hear his stomach growling.

"Coke," he said. Mrs. Avila gave him an afternoon snack which usually held him over until dinner. But sometimes Macky got lost in the midst of her own six children and...

Mrs. Avila! It took Sonya a few moments to realize the depth of her idea. They could wait there, at Mrs. Avila's. And she'd probably have a stack of flour tortillas, fresh off the comal, ready to eat with butter and salt. She grabbed his hand. "Mrs. Avila has Coke."

"Coke!" He jumped up to follow his sister. "Coke," he cooed.

At the major intersection, Sonya quietly calculated their next move while the scores of adults hurried to their own destinations. She scratched one knee as she tried retracing her journey home in the labyrinth of her memory. Things never looked the same when backwards and she searched for familiar scenes. She looked for the newspaperman who sat in a little house with a little T.V. on and sold magazines with naked girls holding beach balls. But he was gone. What remained was a little closet-like shed with chains and locks, and she wondered what happened to him, for she thought he lived there with the naked ladies.

They finally crossed the street at a cautious pace, the colors of the street lights brighter as darkness descended, a stereo store blaring music from two huge, blasting speakers. She thought it was the disco store she passed, but she didn't remember if the sign was green or red. And she didn't remember it flashing like it was now. Studying the neon light, she bumped into a tall, lanky dark man. Maybe it was Raoul's Popi. Raoul was a dark boy in her class that she felt sorry for because everyone called him spongehead. Maybe she could ask Raoul's Popi where Mrs. Avila lived, but before she could think it all out, red sirens flashed in their faces and she shielded her eyes to see the polie.

The polie are men in black who get kids and send them to Tijuana, says Popi. Whenever you see them, run, because they hate you, says Popi. She grabs Macky by his sleeve and they crawl under a table of bargain cassettes. Macky's nose is running, and when he sniffles, she puts her finger to her lips. She peeks from behind the poster of Vincente Fernandez to see Raoul's father putting keys and stuff from his pockets onto the hood of the polie car. And it's true, they're putting him in the car and taking him to Tijuana. Popi, she murmured to herself. Mamá.

"Coke." Macky whispered, as if she had failed to remember.

"Ssssh. Mi'jo, when I say run, you run, okay?" She waited for the tires to turn out, and as the black and white drove off, she whispered "Now," and they scurried out from under the table and ran across the street, oblivious to the horns.

They entered a maze of alleys and dead ends, the long, abandoned warehouses shadowing any light. Macky stumbled and she continued to drag him until his crying, his untied sneakers, and his raspy breathing finally forced her to stop. She scanned the boarded-up boxcars, the rows of rusted rails to make sure the polie wasn't following them. Tired, her heart bursting, she leaned him against a tall chain-link fence. Except for the rambling of some railcars, silence prevailed, and she could hear Macky sniffling in the darkness. Her mouth was parched and she swallowed to rid herself of the

metallic taste of fear. The shadows stalked them, hovering
like nightmares. Across the tracks, in the distance, was a
room with a yellow glow, like a beacon light at the end of a
dark sea. She pinched Macky's nose with the corner of her
dress, took hold of his sleeve. At least the shadows will be
gone, she concluded, at the zero-zero place.

II

Don't look at me. I didn't give it the name. It was passed
on. Didn't even know what it meant until I looked it up in
some library dictionary. But I kinda liked the name. It's, well,
romantic, almost like the name of a song, you know, so I kept
it. That was before JoJo turned fourteen even. But now if you
take a look at the sign, the paint's peeled off 'cept for the two
O's. The double zero cafe. Story of my life. But who cares,
right? As long as everyone 'round the factories knows I run an
honest business.

The place is clean. That's more than I can say for some
people who walk through that door. And I offer the best prices
on double-burger deluxes this side of Main Street. Okay, so
it's not pure beef. Big deal, most meat markets do the same.
But I make no bones 'bout it. I tell them up front, 'yeah, it
ain't dogmeat, but it ain't sirloin either.' Cause that's the sort
of guy I am. Honest.

That's the trouble. It never pays to be honest. I tried
scrubbing the stains off the floor, so that my customers won't
be reminded of what happened. But they keep walking as if
my cafe ain't fit for lepers. And that's the thanks I get for
being a fair guy.

Not once did I hang up all those stupid signs. You know,
like 'We reserve the right to refuse service to anyone,' or 'No
shirt, no shoes, no service.' To tell you the truth—which is
what I always do though it don't pay—I wouldn't have nobody
walking through that door. The streets are full of scum, but
scum gotta eat too is the way I see it. Now, listen. I ain't talking 'bout out-of-luckers, weirdos, whores, you know. I'm talking 'bout five-to-lifers out of some tech. I'm talking Paulie.

I swear Paulie is thirty-five, or six. JoJo's age if he were
still alive, but he don't look a day over ninety. Maybe why I
let him hang out is 'cause he's JoJo's age. Shit, he's okay as
long as he don't bring his wigged-out friends whose voices

sound like a record at low speed. Paulie's got too many stories and they all get jammed up in his mouth so I can't make out what he's saying. He scares the other customers, too, acting like he is shadow boxing, or like a monkey hopping on a frying pan. You know, nervous, jumpy, his jaw all falling and his eyes bulgy and dirt-yellow. I give him the last booth, coffee, and yesterday's donut holes to keep him quiet. After a few minutes, out he goes, before lunch. I'm too old, you know, too busy making ends meet to be nursing the kid. And so is Delia.

That Delia's got these unique titties. One is bigger than the other. Like an orange and grapefruit. I kid you not. They're like that on account of when she was real young she had some babies, and they all sucked only one favorite tittie. So one is bigger than the other, and when she used to walk in with Paulie, huggy-huggy and wearing those tight leotard blouses that show the nipple dots, you could see the difference. You could tell right off that Paulie was proud of them, the way he'd hang his arm over her shoulder and squeeze the grapefruit. They kill me, her knockers. She'd come in real queen-like, smacking gum and chewing the fat with the illegals who work in that garment warehouse. They come in real queen-like, too, sitting in the best booth near the window, and order cokes. That's all. Cokes. Hey, but I'm a nice guy. So what if they mess up my table, bring their own lunches and only order small cokes, leaving a dime as tip? So sometimes the place ain't crawling with people, you comprende, buddy? A dime's a dime as long as it's in my pocket.

Like I gotta pay my bills, too. I gotta eat. So like I serve anybody who's got the greens, including that crazy lady and the two kids that started all the trouble. If only I had closed early. But I had to wash the dinner dishes on account of I can't afford a dishwasher. I was scraping off some birdshit glue stuck to this plate, see, when I hear the bells jingle against the door. I hate those fucking bells. That was Nell's idea. Nell's my wife; my ex-wife. So people won't sneak up on you, says my ex. Anyway, I'm standing behind the counter staring at this short woman. Already I know that she's bad news because she looks street to me. Round face, burnt-toast color, black hair that hangs like straight ropes. Weirdo, I've had enough to last me a lifetime. She's wearing a shawl and a dirty slip is hanging out. Shit if I have to dish out a free meal. Funny thing, but I didn't see the two kids 'til I got to the

booth. All of a sudden I see these big eyes looking over the
table's edge at me. It shook me up, the way they kinda
appeared. Aw, maybe they were there all the time.

The boy's a sweetheart. Short Order don't look nothing
like his mom. He's got dried snot all over his dirty cheeks and
his hair ain't seen a comb for years. She can't take care of herself, much less him or the doggie of a sister. But he's a tough
one, and I pinch his nose 'cause he's a real sweetheart like
JoJo. You know, my boy.

It's his sister I don't like. She's got these poking eyes that
follow you 'round 'cause she don't trust no one. Like when I
reach for Short Order, she flinches like I'm 'bout to tear his
nose off, gives me a nasty, squinty look. She's maybe five,
maybe six, I don't know, and she acts like she owns him. Even
when I bring the burgers, she doesn't let go of his hand.
Finally, the fellow bites it and I wink at him. A real sweetheart.

In the next booth, I'm twisting the black crud off the top
of the ketchup bottle when I hear the lady saying something
in Spanish. Right off I know she's illegal, which explains why
she looks like a weirdo. Anyway, she says something nice to
them 'cause it's in the same tone that Nell used when I'd rest
my head on her lap. I'm surprised the illegal's got a fiver to
pay, but she and her tail leave no tip. I see Short Order's
small bites on the bun.

You know, a cafe's the kinda business that moves. You
get some regulars, but most of them are on the move, so I
don't pay much attention to them. But this lady's face sticks
like egg yolk on a plate. It ain't 'til I open a beer and sit in
front of the B & W to check out the wrestling matches that I
see this news bulletin 'bout two missing kids. I recognize the
mugs right away. Short Order and his doggie sister. And all of
a sudden her face is out of my mind. Aw, fuck, I say, and put
my beer down so hard that the foam spills onto last month's
Hustler. Aw, fuck.

See, if Nell was here, she'd know what to do: call the cops.
But I don't know. Cops ain't exactly my friends, and all I need
is for bacon to be crawling all over my place. And seeing how
her face is vague now, I decide to wait 'til the late news. Short
Order don't look right neither. I'll have another beer and wait
for the late news. The alarm rings at four and I have this
headache, see, from the sixpack, and I gotta get up. I was sup-

posed to do something, but I got all suck-faced and forgot. Turn off the T.V., take a shower, but that don't help my memory any.

Hear sirens near the railroad tracks. Cops. I'm supposed to call the cops. I'll do it after I make the coffee, put away the eggs, get the donuts out. But Paulie strolls in looking partied out. We actually talk 'bout last night's wrestling match between BoBo Brazil and the Crusher. I slept through it, you see. Paulie orders an O.J. on account of he's catching a cold. I open up my big mouth and ask about De. Drinks the rest of his O.J., says real calm-like, that he caught her eaglespread with the vegetable fatso down the block. Then, very polite-like, Paulie excuses himself. That's one thing I gotta say about Paulie. He may be one big Fuck-Up, but he's got manners. Juice gave him shit cramps, he says.

Well, leave it to Paulie. Good ole Mr. Fuck-Up himself to help me with the cops. The prick O.D.'s in my crapper; vomits and shits are all over—I mean all over the fuckin' walls. That's the thanks I get for being Mr. Nice Guy. I had the cops looking up my ass for the stash. Says one, the one wearing a mortician's suit, We'll be back, we'll be back when you ain't looking. If I was pushing, would I be burning my goddamn balls off with spitting grease? So fuck 'em, I think. I ain't gonna tell you nothing 'bout the lady. Fuck you, I say to them as they drive away. Fuck your mother.

That's why Nell was good to have 'round. She could be a pain in the ass, you know, like making me hang those stupid bells, but mostly she knew what to do. See, I go bananas. Like my mind fries with the potatoes and by the end of the day, I'm deader than dogshit. Let me tell you what I mean. A few hours later, after I swore I wouldn't give the fuckin' pigs the time of day, the green vans roll up across the street. While I'm stirring the chili con carne, I see all these illegals running out of the factory to hide, like roaches when the lightswitch goes on. I taste the chile, but I really can't taste nothing on account of I've lost my appetite after cleaning out the crapper, when three of them run into the Cariboo. They look at me as if I'm gonna stop them, but when I go on stirring the chile, they run to the bathroom. Now look, I'm a nice guy, but I don't like to be used, you know? Just 'cause they're regulars don't mean jackshit. I run an honest business. And that's what I told them agents. See, by that time, my stomach being all dizzy,

and the cops all over the place, and the three illegals running
in here, I was all confused, you know. That's how it was, and
well, I haven't seen Nell for years, and I guess that's why I
pointed to the bathroom.

I don't know. I didn't expect handcuffs and them agents
putting their hands up and down their thighs. When they
walked passed me, they didn't look at me. That is, the two
young ones. The older one, the one that looked silly in the
handcuffs on account of she's old enough to be my grandma's
grandma, looks straight at my face with the same eyes Short
Order's sister gave me yesterday. What a day. Then, to top off
the potatoes with the gravy, the bells jingle against the door
and in enters the lady again with the two kids.

III

He's got lice. Probably from living in the detainers. Those
are the rooms where they round up the children and make
them work for their food. I saw them from the window. Their
eyes are cut glass, and no one looks for sympathy. They take
turns, sorting out the arms from the legs, heads from the tor-
sos. Is that one your mother? one guard asks, holding a mum-
mified head with eyes shut tighter than coffins. But the
children no longer cry. They just continue sorting as if they
were salvaging cans from a heap of trash. They do this until
time is up and they drift into a tunnel, back to the womb of
sleep, while a new group comes in. It is all very organized. I
bite my fist to keep from retching. Please, God, please don't
let Geraldo be there.

For you see, they took Geraldo. By mistake, of course. It
was my fault. I shouldn't have sent him out to fetch me a
mango. But it was just to the corner. I didn't even bother to
put his sweater on. I hear his sandals flapping against the
gravel. I follow him with my eyes, see him scratching his buttocks when the wind picks up swiftly, as it often does at such
unstable times, and I have to close the door.

The darkness becomes a serpent's tongue, swallowing us
whole. It is the night of La Llorona. The women come up from
the depths of sorrow to search for their children. I join them,
frantic, desperate, and our eyes become scrutinizers, our bodies opiated with the scent of their smiles. Descending from
door to door, the wind whips our faces. I hear the wailing of

the women and know it to be my own. Geraldo is nowhere to be found.

Dawn is not welcomed. It is a drunkard wavering between consciousness and sleep. My life is fleeing, moving south towards the sea. My tears are now hushed and faint.

The boy, barely a few years older than Geraldo, lights a cigarette, rests it on the edge of his desk, next to all the other cigarette burns. The blinds are down to keep the room cool. Above him hangs a single bulb that shades and shadows his face in such a way as to mask his expressions. He is not to be trusted. He fills in the information, for I cannot write. Statements delivered, we discuss motives.

"Spies," says he, flicking a long burning ash from the cigarette onto the floor, then wolfing the smoke in as if his lungs had an unquenchable thirst for nicotine. "We arrest spies. Criminals." He says this with cigarette smoke spurting out from his nostrils like a nosebleed. "Spies? Criminal?" My shawl falls to the ground. "He is only five and a half years old." I plead for logic with my hands. "What kind of crimes could a five-year-old commit?"

"Anyone who so willfully supports the Contras in any form must be arrested and punished without delay." He knows the line by heart. I think about moths and their stupidity. Always attracted by light, they fly into fires, or singe their wings with the heat of the single bulb and fall on his desk, writhing in pain. I don't understand why nature has been so cruel as to prevent them from feeling warmth. He dismisses them with a sweep of a hand. "This," he continues, "is what we plan to do with the Contras and those who aid them." He inhales again.

"But, Señor, he's just a baby."

"Contras are tricksters. They exploit the ignorance of people like you. Perhaps they convinced your son to circulate pamphlets. You should be talking to them, not us." The cigarette is down to his yellow finger tips, to where he can no longer continue to hold it without burning himself. He throws the stub on the floor, crushes it under his boot. "This," he says, screwing his boot into the ground, "is what the Contras do to people like you."

"Señor. I am a washerwoman. You yourself see I cannot read or write. There is my X. Do you think my son can read?" How can I explain to this man that we are poor, that we live as best we can? "If such a thing has happened, perhaps he wanted to make a few centavos for his mamá. He's just a baby."

"So you are admitting his guilt?"

"So you are admitting he is here?" I promise, once I see him, hold him in my arms again, I will never, never scold him for wanting more than I can give. "You see, he needs his sweater... " The sweater lies limp on my lap.

"Your assumption is incorrect."

"May I check the detainers for myself?"

"In time."

"And what about my Geraldo?"

"In time." He dismisses me, placing the forms in a big envelope crinkled by the day's humidity.

"When?" I am wringing the sweater with my hands.

"Don't be foolish, woman. Now off with your nonsense. We will try to locate your Pedro."

"Geraldo."

Maria came by today with a bowl of hot soup. She reports, in her usual excited way, that the soldiers are now eating the brains of their victims. It is unlike her to be so scandalous. So insane. Geraldo must be cold without his sweater.

"Why?" I ask as the soup gets cold. I will write Tavo tonight.

At the plaza, a group of people are whispering. They are quiet when I pass, turn to one another and put their finger to their lips to cage their voices. They continue as I reach the church steps. To be associated with me is condemnation.

Today I felt like killing myself, Lord. But I am too much of a coward. I am a washerwoman, Lord. My mother was one, and hers, too. We have lived as best we can, washing other people's laundry, rinsing off other people's dirt until our hands crust and chap. When my son wanted to hold my hand, I held soap instead. When he wanted to play, my feet were in pools of water. It takes such little courage, being a washerwoman. Give me strength, Lord.

What have I done to deserve this, Lord? Raising a child is like building a kite. You must bend the twigs enough, but not too much, for you might break them. You must find paper that is delicate and light enough to wave on the breath of the wind, yet must withstand the ravages of a storm. You must tie the strings gently but firmly so that it may not fall apart. You must let the string go, eventually, so that the kite will stretch its ambition. It is such delicate work, Lord, being a mother. This I understand, Lord, because I am. But you have snapped the cord, Lord. It was only a matter of minutes and my life is lost somewhere in the clouds. I don't know, I don't know what games you play, Lord.

These four walls are no longer my house; the earth beneath it, no longer my home. Weeds have replaced all good crops. The irrigation ditches are clodded with bodies. No matter where we turn, there are rumors facing us, and we try to live as best we can under the rule of men who rape women then rip their fetuses form their bellies. Is this our home? Is this our country? I ask Maria. Don't these men have mothers, lovers, babies, sisters? Don't they see what they are doing? Later, Maria says, these men are babes farted out from the Devil's ass. We check to make sure no one has heard her say this.

Without Geraldo, this is not my home; the earth beneath it, not my country. This is why I have to leave. Maria begins to cry. Not because I am going, but because she is staying.

Tavo. Sweet Tavo. He has sold his car to send me the money. He has just married and he sold his car for me. Thank you, Tavo. Not just for the money. But also for making me believe in the goodness of people again...The money is enough to buy off the border soldiers. The rest will come from the can. I have saved for Geraldo's schooling and it is enough for a bus ticket to Juarez. I am to wait for Tavo there.

I spit. I do not turn back.

Perhaps I am wrong in coming. I worry that Geraldo will not have a home to return to, no mother to cradle his nightmares away, soothe the scars, stop the hemorrhaging of his heart. Tavo is happy I am here, but it is crowded with the three of us, and I hear them arguing behind their closed door. There is only so much a nephew can provide. I must find work. I have two hands willing to work. But the heart. The heart wills only to watch the children playing in the street.

The machines, their speed and dust, make me ill. But I can clean. I clean toilets, dump trash cans, sweep. Disinfect the sinks. I will gladly do whatever is necessary to repay Tavo. The baby is due any time and money is tight. I volunteer for odd hours, weekends, since I really have very little to do. When the baby comes, I know Tavo's wife will not let me hold it, for she thinks I am a bad omen. I know it.

Why would God play such a cruel joke, if he isn't my son? I jumped the curb, dashed out into the street, but the street is becoming wider and wider. I've lost him once and can't lose him again and to hell with the screeching tires and the horns and the headlights barely touching my hips. I can't take my eyes off him because, you see, they are swift and cunning and can take your life with a snap of a finger. But God is a just man and His mistakes can be undone.

My heart pounds in my head like a sledgehammer against the asphalt. What if it isn't Geraldo? What if he is still in the detainer waiting for me? A million questions, one answer: Yes. Geraldo, yes. I want to touch his hand first, have it disappear in my own because it is so small. His eyes look at me in total bewilderment. I grab him because the earth is crumbling beneath us and I must save him. We both fall to the ground.

A hot meal is in store. A festival. The cook, a man with shrunken cheeks and the hands of a car mechanic, takes a liking to Geraldo. Its like birthing you again, mi'jo. My baby.

I bathe him. He flutters in excitement, the water gray around him. I scrub his head with lye to kill off the lice, comb his hair out with a fine-tooth comb. I wash his rubbery penis, wrap him in a towel, and he stands in front of the window, shriveling and sucking milk from a carton, his hair shiny from the dampness.

He finally sleeps. So easily, she thinks. On her bed next to the open window he coos in the night. Below, the sounds of the city become as monotonous as the ocean waves. She rubs his back with warm oil, each stroke making up for the days of his absence. She hums to him softly so that her breath brushes against his face, tunes that are rusted and crack in her throat. The hotel neon shines on his back and she covers him.

All the while the young girl watches her brother sleeping. She removes her sneakers, climbs into the bed, snuggles up to her brother, and soon her breathing is raspy, her arms under her stomach.

The couch is her bed tonight. Before switching the light off, she checks once more to make sure this is not a joke. Tomorrow she will make arrangements to go home. Maria will be the same, the mango stand on the corner next to the church plaza will be the same. It will all be the way it was before. But enough excitement. For the first time in years, her mind is quiet of all noise and she has the desire to sleep.

The bells jingle when the screen door slaps shut behind them. The cook wrings his hands in his apron, looking at them. Geraldo is in the middle, and they sit in the booth farthest away from the window, near the hall where the toilets are, and right away the small boy, his hair now neatly combed and split to the side like an adult, wrinkles his nose at the peculiar smell. The cook wipes perspiration off his forehead with the corner of his apron, finally comes over to the table.

She looks so different, so young. Her hair is combed slick back into one thick braid and her earrings hang like baskets of golden pears on her finely sculptured ears. He can't believe how different she looks. Almost beautiful. She points to what she wants on the menu with a white, clean fingernail. Although confused, the cook is sure of one thing—it's Short Order all right, pointing to him with a commanding finger, saying his only English word: coke.

His hands tremble as he slaps the meat on the grill; the patties hiss instantly. He feels like vomiting. The chile overboils and singes the fires, deep red trail of chile crawling to the floor and puddling there. He grabs the handles, burns himself, drops the pot on the wooden racks of the floor. He sucks his fingers, the patties blackening and sputtering grease. He flips them, and the burgers hiss anew. In some strange way he hopes they have disappeared, and he takes a quick look only to see Short Order's sister, still in the same dress, still holding her brother's hand. She is craning her neck to peek at what is going on in the kitchen.

Aw, fuck, he says, in a fog of smoke, his eyes burning tears. He can't believe it, but he's crying. For the first time since JoJo's death, he's crying. He becomes angry at the lady for returning. At JoJo. At Nell for leaving him. He wishes Nell here, but doesn't know where she's at or what part of Vietnam JoJo is all crumbled up in. Children gotta be with their parents, family gotta be together, he thinks. It's only right. The emergency line is ringing.

Two black and whites roll up and skid the front tires against the curb. The flashing lights carousel inside the cafe.

She sees them opening the screen door, their guns taught and
cold like steel erections. Something is wrong, and she looks to
the cowering cook. She has been betrayed, and her heart is
pounding like footsteps running, faster, louder, faster, and
she can't hear what they are saying to her. She jumps up from
the table, grabs Geraldo by the wrist, his sister dragged along
because, like her, she refuses to release his hand. Their lips
are mouthing words she can't hear, can't comprehend. Run,
Run is all she can think of to do, Run through the hallway,
out to the alley, Run because they will never take him away
again.

But her legs are heavy and she crushes Geraldo against
her, so tight, as if she wants to conceal him in her body again,
return him to her belly so that they will not castrate him and
hang his small blue penis on her door, not crush his face so
that he is unrecognizable, not bury him among the heaps of
bones, and ears, and teeth, and jaws, because no one but she
cared to know that he cried. For years he cried and she could
hear him day and night. Screaming, howling, sobbing, shriveling and crying because he is only five years old, and all she
wanted was a mango.

But the crying begins all over again. In the distance, she
hears crying.

She refuses to let go. For they will have to cut her arms
off to take him, rip her mouth off to keep her from screaming
for help. Without thinking, she reaches over to where two
pots of coffee are brewing and throws the steaming coffee into
their faces. Outside, people begin to gather, pressing their
faces against the window glass to get a good view. The cook
huddles behind the counter, frightened, trembling. Their
faces become distorted and she doesn't see the huge hand that
takes hold of Geraldo and she begins screaming all over
again, screaming so that the walls shake, screaming enough
for all the women of murdered children, screaming, pleading
for help from the people outside, and she pushes an open
hand against an officer's nose, because no one will stop them
and he pushes the gun barrel to her face.

And I laugh at his ignorance. How stupid of him to think
that I will let them take my Geraldo away just because he
waves that gun like a flag. Well, to hell with you, you pieces of
shit, do you hear me? Stupid, cruel pigs. To hell with you all,
because you can no longer frighten me. I will fight you for my

son until I have no hands left to hold a knife. I will fight you all because you're all farted out of the Devil's ass, and you'll not take us with you. I am laughing, howling at their stupidity because they should know by now that I will never let my son go. And then I hear something crunching like broken glass against my forehead and I am blinded by the liquid darkness. But I hold onto his hand. That I can feel, you see, I'll never let go. Because we are going home. My son and I.

The Long
Reconciliation

The Long Reconciliation

I

Blowing with the passion of a trumpet player, Chato wipes the hairs of his nose clean. His favorite handkerchief with embroidered initials is soiled, ragged, now moist, but he folds it with the care of a mother diapering her first born. He thinks, Age is a Vampiress. Feeling the pin pains inside him and the tremors of stubborn phlegm in his chest, he puts the handkerchief in his right back pocket. Another cough suppressed, bones settling, he resumes his motionless position.

He nests on a crate with his hands resting on a flyswatter which lies across his lap. The flies, buzzing wildly, fail to disturb him because the carousel is about to begin. He feels the bells, the colors. The music pulsates his fingers into galloping horses. Sitting erect on his horse, he stops to survey the newly bought land. The dust reaches him and he covers his nose with a handkerchief until it settles and clears, and he sees himself carefully inspecting the land. Sporadic bushes and defiant spines of yucca are all he sees, survivors of a ravenous land. So this is home, is all he thinks to himself, home. *Within him, his heart mirrored the pulsating kitchen of his home where she freely dwelled, thawing his blood; within her, a seed, his love, their child, became undone, within the eggplant womb; secretly crawling down one thigh, voiceless, like a mute; returning home, now, like his son, to the heartland* and Chato loses himself in the abysmal jar, reaching for his child's unborn face.

Son? Have you arrived or is it that you have yet to leave? Sprout your ear and listen to the carousel music bounce like bubbles in the air. Circle, turn, whirl and whirlpool dizzy with sticky hairs was my birth, but now the pool is a vacuum—my legs dangle, my fingers tire of gripping the edge. The veins in my arms escape as thick hospital tubes. Child?

Chato?
My son?
Your wife.
Go to hell, Chato.
Let me be.
Do you know what it is like to die, my husband?
I died long before you were buried, woman.
Then we die differently, you and I?
What do you want of me? You have already destroyed
what I loved more than you.
And you, Chato?
I killed for honor.
Then I killed for life. It's the same thing, isn't it? Which is
worse? You killed because something said: 'you must kill to
remain a man—and not for this honor. For me, things are as
different as our bodies. I killed, as you say, because it would
have been unbearable to watch a child slowly rot. But you
couldn't understand that because something said 'you must
have sons to remain a man.'
Amanda. I am poor. This earth bore me to live, to have
children, to die, and it is not for me to change it. But you, you
changed it and closed the door to my sunlight. Now, I die with
pain knowing that all I will have left as a sign of my life is a
stonemark without a name. I die alone.
The bells of music stab the temples of his head and he
feels the gravel, rough like sandpaper on his cheek. Chato has
fallen off the crate. He feels footsteps around him, muffled
voices and he opens his eyes to see them hovering like shadows of birds, and he faintly hears his bones clattering as they
lift him. A dead fly is impressed on his cheek and a hand
wipes it away. The blanket is cold; he knows they have taken
his trousers off. He will die alone.
Touch my hand, Chato. Forgive and die with me.
Chato sees himself get off his horse and grab a handful of
land. Grainy dust. Home. The priest had told him to save
every penny. Land is valuable, and you can at least grow a
livelihood for you and your family. It is a hope, Chato remembers the priest saying. And he did save every penny except for
the gifts he bought Amanda. The carousel, so expensive. That
day he tells Amanda of the land he has not seen yet. This is
the first time he has spoken to his wife in a long, long time,
and he sees her surprise when he mentions the name

Joaquín. Or perhaps she is surprised about the land. Chato sees himself, excited— trying to hide the excitement, and for a moment he feels like touching her, his wife. Perhaps, after he builds the house they will begin another life together. Before, Amanda would touch him and try to make him love her again. Each time she touched him, he saw his child's face, and would jerk away from her grasp. He remembers even crying once, behind the house in the dark. Perhaps later, but now he has promised himself and he walks away, his spurs loud on the wooden porch. Grainy dust. He sees Don Joaquín approaching, his horse trotting confidently.

You acted like God, Amanda. I acted like a man should.

"Chato! How do you like the land? Practically given to you! Look, just to the south of here, you can set up irrigation ditches and..."

"It's desert."

"Excuse my laughter, but what did you expect for the few pennies you've given me?"

"I've given you everything I'm worth...without being castrated."

"And I've given you what you're worth, my friend. Desert!"

Chato sees himself surrounded by people who thicken like nervous ants as he brings Don Joaquín in. Mouths first murmur sentences, now shout words, while the cool bursts of breeze gently dry the drooling saliva from the dying man. The voices follow them to Chato's porch. After the doctor leaves, Amanda Márquez prays near Don Joaquín. Chato has surrendered his bed and his wife to this man, and he sits quietly on a crate viewing the mountains from the next room. He turns to his wife, who holds a heavy rosary, then returns to the mountains, where into a blissful sleep he can see his heart smiling.

He remembers his heart smiling.

He remembers his mother's crumbling voice calling for him: "Chato." The word with no emphasis, just an empty "Chato" almost cursed, her son the runt boy who learned to hoe the land at three and could sing passionate corridos about men impoverished by love, men scorned or continuously intoxicated, like the clown who was the proprietor of the yearly event in the village, the carousel with its bells and rings enticing all the filthy children to steal, beg, hunt for centavos

to hop on the painted wooden horses going nowhere but making little ragged puffed-cheeked children cheer and laugh for
three minutes like they were kings, landowners, savoring
every morsel of the carousel's delight, proud of their majestic
selves for three minutes until the carousel slowed to a stop
and then the children cherished the memory beneath their
fast-pacing hearts...hungrier.

And "Chato" was the soft breath of Amanda Márquez at
the tender age of fourteen whispering penetration, and the
moon was her first gift to him, gleaming raw that night when
he presented himself to her family, telling them that his love
would make up for her lack of it, and hearing her father laugh
at him with a laugh that comes from deep inside saying "She's
a jewel," grabbing her by the arm and laughing out loud
knowing how ugly she was, but only to her family because
Chato loved her so much that he bought her a small carousel
to keep in the new house he would build for her, and he also
promised her father (while she looked on in amazement at the
carousel he held in one hand and the two red apples he held
in the other) that he, Chato, would be as virile as the land he
would buy. But all her father did was laugh at him, his viril-
ity, his dream, with a laugh that locked itself somewhere
inside Chato; laughed that same, heavy boisterous laugh Don
Joaquín laughed just before he, Chato, struck him with a
knife, cutting him like butter. He was so soft, this man whom
Amanda hated for no reason at all except she kept saying to
the dying man, you told him, you told him, and Chato
watched her as she prayed for him, and when she lifted herself up from kneeling, he watched her float into the next room
where he, Chato, sat, going outside with an empty jar to
where the heat had transformed the garbage into tireless
maggots. And Chato wanted to stop her, wanted to ask Why
are you doing this, watching her come inside the house, like
an apparition, going over to where Don Joaquín was breathing heavily, and with her filthy hands Chato watched her
force open the newly mended wound and he can almost hear
the delicate tearing of each stitch plucking one by one, seeing
her, his wife, Amanda, crazy with hate, put the bigger worms
in his body to let him rot before his death, watching her
replace the gauze neatly, then kneeling to pray once again for
this man Don Joaquín, and the carousel is quiet in his heart.

II

"The cock will pluck the hen tonight."

"Ah, Chato, my friend, how many sons will you sire? Five? Six? Can you even father one, you son of a bitch!"

"She is big-hipped. She will carry many children."

"Always stand up. That way you won't get pregnant. Look at me, only seven!!"

"Full-moon children are born with horns."

"Let's see you kiss the bride."

"...then I took off my pants and I told her, 'Now you put them on,' and she did. Then I said, 'See! The pants fit me, not you. Don't forget that it's me who wears them...'"

Only with an escaping nervous laugh did she open her mouth to reveal slightly enlarged gums. And Amanda was nervous. And excited. And frightened by the new arrangement, this idea of marriage. Her family called her wild, like the jackrabbits, timid, not strong, but strong-willed, and none expected her to marry. But married she was to a stranger nearly twice her age.

In one breath she drifted from the priest, with his matrimonial rosary chains linking them together until death, to the reception where the neighborhood men with their ribboned guitars played music that jumped with dance steps and where she smeared her dress with chile, to finally her husband's crusty rooms.

The rooms were humid until she started the fire. With a stove, table, two chairs, shelves and the bed she sat on, it was a house not yet a home and her duty was made clear by the light of the fire burning. Amanda heard the hoofs of his horse, then the creak from the saddle seating a man heavy with drink. She heard his spurs reach the wooden porch; an unsteady pace. The pace receded and became cushioned with distance as he reached the end of the porch, louder as he approached the door, then receded again. Finally, the pacing stopped and she heard him strike a match, imagining him lighting his cigar. She jumped from the bed when the door swung open. He stood there, immobile. To the back of him lay the dry, cold flatlands, thin with hunger. In front of him stood Amanda, frightened, pure, her skin brown and rich like the fertile soil, like the fruitful earth should be, his heartland, only hope, now his wife, amidst the warmth of the fire.

His hand was like ice on her budding breasts, and he
pinched her nipples gently. Amanda was terrified. Unable to
move, mesmerized by the sensation of his fingers, she closed
her eyes and tried to imagine death. The pain was too great,
her mother said, she must bear it, clench your teeth, children
are made by pain, her mother said, children are born by pain,
but she felt the softness of lips touch the sides of her body, as
soft as a cat's walk. That night he said her name a thousand
times without sounds, probing her until his fingers were lost
somewhere in maiden hair. The storm came as a surprise, the
tropical rainfall between her legs, then he came hard and wet,
with a grunt close to her ear.

Amanda lay there thinking of the moistness, the itch. He
finally turned away to sleep, and she thought, so this is love,
reaching down to contact her undiscovered island which
Chato had just claimed as his own. She brought her moistened fingers up to her nose. So this, she thought, was the
smell of love. Raising the same hand up to the moonlight, she
spotted red fingers. The moon was red. She woke Chato.

"Chato," she said, "I'm no longer a child. Look." She held
her hand for him to see.

"You're still a child," he said, "but one that can bear children."

*God didn't listen to me, and neither did you, Chato. You
are as guilty as I am.*

"Anita, the young couple, they have been married for
three months with no word of children."

"Comadre, the first three months of a child are quiet
ones. She is probably on her fourth month now."

"If that is so, Anita, then tell me why she is visiting Don
Serafín, God help him? She is dry, that's why! What sadness.
So young, so useless."

"What's this? Visits with the devil himself? May God in
heaven save us all. When did you hear of this?"

"I…well…the curtains are thin in the confessional booths."

"God save us, you heard Amanda's sins, Comadre?"

"How could I help it, Anita, I was next in line?"

"May God forgive you for listening. What did the jackrab-
bit say? Comes to Church only when she needs God's help."

"Only this: something about problems, something about
corn-silk tea, something about Don Serafín. Then, Señora
Ramírez enters carrying her youngest, and for no reason the

child begins screaming like a soul in hell. I couldn't hear another word."

"So young, so useless. And to think your daughter would have been just right for Chato."

"So young. But she doesn't have half the problems Señora Ramírez has, you know, married to a drunk and all..."

Amanda saw the two women cackling on the front steps of the church. She had lit two candles for the Holy Virgin and she came out just in time to see the two stop and stare at her. She bowed out of custom to them and began her half-mile walk towards her house, hoping to get there before the deep dark. She walked quickly, recognizing the different houses and paths. When she passed the great white house, she saw Don Joaquín sitting on the porch with bare feet. Were he not living alone at the time, the barking of the dogs would have awakened the household. He saw her small image and waved for her to come in. Amanda, wrapped in her rebozo, quickly walked away, disappearing like the dreams he often had of her. As he lay down, Don Joaquín promised himself he would have to see her again.

She remembered. It is so hard being female, Amanda, and you must understand that that is the way it was meant to be, *said the priest in the confessional.* But this is pain, Father, to sprout a child that we can't feed or care for. Pray, pray, pray, *said the priest,* but what is a poor Amanda to do? The moon has hidden its face many times and I still have yet to bleed. Dried orange peels, and even corn-silk tea, will stir the blood to flow, *said Don Serafín.* Each morning I wait. Just drink the tea, drink it.

Each morning is drearier than the last. To awake and feel something inside draining you. Lying on my back, I can almost see where all my energy is going, below my navel, where my hair stops. It will be soon, *he said.* I stroke it to calm its hunger, but it won't be satisfied until it gets all of me. Then he wants me. Amanda, Amanda, I love to hold you, to love you, *said Chato.* He likes mornings. I lie there rubbing my belly while he kneads my breasts. I know what he wants and I hide the sickness from him. But Father, wasn't He supposed to take care of us, His poor? When you lie together, it is for creating children, *said the priest.* You have sinned, pray. Sex is the only free pleasure we have. It makes us feel like clouds for the minutes that not even you can prevent. You ask us not to lie together, but we are not made of you, we are not gods. You, God, eating and drinking as you like, you, there, not feeling the sweat or the pests that feed on the skin, you sitting with a kingly lust for comfort, tell us that we will be paid later on in death. Amanda, Amanda, I love you, *said Chato*. Listen to me, condemn me to hell, to this life, to anything, but please, please, let me not be pregnant. It will be soon.

"You make me crazy. Get up! Look at your dress. Howling like a coyote!"

She trembled with misery as he led her into the house. The kitchen was dark except for one candle on the table which flickered their phantom images on the walls. She sat, staring into the candle while he prepared some herbs and water. Numbly, she opened her mouth slowly with each teaspoon he fed her.

"The moon's face is hidden again," she said between teaspoons, still looking at the candle as her tears rolled down like the melted wax along the candlestick. Beads of sweat formed on his face. Why is it that he could never understand her? The moon's face is hidden? She sees it. I see it, but I find her howling like a coyote, fighting in the dirt. At what? The faceless moon? What the devil is happening to you? What is causing you so much pain?

He watched her turn into a hurricane in the darkness. She threw up the meal she could not afford to, shattered dishes, and overturned the small kitchen table. Winded, she collapsed on the floor, sobbing until her eyes were swollen.

As confused and afraid as he was when he first held a rabbit, he held her. She was carried into the next room where she was gently laid on the bed, strands of hair removed from her face, and a blanket thrown over her trembling body. She heard him fumbling through some boxes in the closet and she turned to find him holding the carousel.

"Children die like crops here," she said. But he could not hear her, for the bells of carousel music came forth sounding like an orchestra in the silence of the night.

III

He watched her breasts quiver each time she wiped the small creaky tables around him, and he viewed them with slow admiration. Don Joaquín was alone, except for her, in the one-room cantina where the wooden floor planks were covered with dust, and drank mescal from a clay mug, swallowing the stinging clear liquor fast. He pounded his empty mug on the table, startling her, he enjoying her fright, her breasts quivering as she scrambled over to the bar and returned to his table, flicking her long hair over her shoulder.

The woman felt his blurry red eyes burn holes into her skin and she thought, You lonely, lonely coward; if you need a woman, marry a local, share your money. She noticed his beard speckled with grey and thought, Or drink your nights and what's left of your youth away.

At first he pictured himself feeling her bare hips, suckling those delicious breasts, but now, while she stood there pouring the mescal, he hated the woman because she was dull like worn bronze. Her hair, her face, especially her eyes, reflected the sameness of everyday, the waste—and he hated. Before, he was comforted with books, but here, people were puzzled with his words, his knowledge. Later, he turned to women. Now he was content to drink.

Don Joaquín puffed on his second cigar while playing with a splinter from a table which bit into his finger and caused blood beads. I'll be damned, he muttered, bringing his finger closer, and he wedged out the splinter with the point of his knife. With one last gulp he finished the mescal and listened, his hand still cupping the mug, to the cushioned sounds of dogs barking at the men walking home from the fields. Don't you get tired of eating the dust that belongs to someone else's land? he thought. The slow burn of the evening sun created a slab of light on the table where he sat watching the men proceed home, their shadow passing the window. His finger bled. Of going home to dull-eyed wives and filthy, ignorant children that look just like you?

"Señor," the woman said, "your finger. It bleeds. Put this, like this, around it." She handed him a handkerchief with her initials, and he recognized the design and touched the embroidery lightly. "Señora Márquez. She makes beautiful handkerchiefs, pillow cases, scarves, just you ask her," the woman said, watching him, he silent. The clang of a single bell signaled the beginning of evening Mass, and soon the light slab on the table melted into the approaching night. His legs were outstretched and crossed at the ankles, his cigar burning a dark spot on the edge of the table. The woman still watched him, from the bar now, as he gazed into the graying horizon. He is not here, she thought. Perhaps he is in the rich valleys of Zacatecas, running through the green fields as a boy. Or is this rich son in colleges up north, states united? This man, he can return to those places anytime, but why always return here, to drink and burn my tables?

As Don Joaquín got up to leave, he asked the woman her name.

"Does it matter?" she asked.

"No. I guess not," he replied. Don Joaquín staggered to his horse, burping the liquor. The mass was over and he saw two women on the church steps talking as he heaved onto the saddle. When he reached the porch of his home, he fell. The dogs licked his face while he sat on the steps, his hand slipping several times before he was able to remove his boots. He thought he had first imagined her, but when the dogs began barking, he knew it was her and he waved for her to come. Amanda, wrapped in her rebozo, quickly walked away, disappearing—like the dreams he often had of her. As he lay down, Don Joaquín promised himself he would have to see her again.

Mouths first murmur sentences, now shout words. Liberator, they call him as he brings Don Joaquín in while the cool bursts of breeze gently dry the drooling saliva from the dying man.

Right before the dawning, the kitchen fires glowed from the window across the village. The women woke first to prepare tacos of tortillas and beans wrapped in cloth for lunch. Then the men woke, groggy, achey, quietly eating their tortilla and salt, with or without chile. Their lunch in one hand, their tools in the other, they walked to the fields, the older ones with their skin of leather and maps of age on their faces; the younger ones, like Chato, hopeful still, not yet resigned. And they talked, these vague images of men at dawn. They talked in low voices about a thing going on beyond their village, a revolution. There was a plan, a young one said, by some indio, to divide the lands and give it to landless people. Does that mean the death of the likes of Don Joaquín? asked an older one, his voice crumbling. Talk, all talk, Chato thought. He had finally saved enough to pay down on a piece

of land, and he saved every penny because he did not believe
in talk, or the revolution, or for that matter, God.
The voices follow them to Chato's porch. The revolu-
tionary, they say, the honorable liberator of the village. The
mountains will be your home now.

At midday, Don Joaquín inspected the progression of
work from a hill overlooking the fields. He could barely see
the workers eating gathered together under a tree. He
remembered the woman in the cantina. No. It really didn't
matter that he knew her name, and it really didn't matter
that he knew the workers' names. They were all the same. He
signaled to the foreman with a whistle. Nothing really mat-
tered much. After giving instructions, he rode off to the cantina, the foreman watching the clouds of dust carried away by
the breeze.

You told him, you told him, she kept telling the dying
man, holding the heavy rosary and praying for his death.

The woman swore at the misfortune of him coming
through the doors of the cantina, and she handed him the
mug of mescal before he went to his usual table near the window. "Señor," she said, "you took it, my handkerchief." And
she held out her hand.

"Señorita," he said, "where does this Señora Márquez
live?"

Chato has surrendered his bed and his wife to this dying
man, and he sits quietly on a crate viewing the mountains
from the next room where into a blissful sleep he can see his
heart smiling.

For months, Don Joaquín came to the back door after
Chato left to work the fields, ready with comfort, eager to
please, rusting Amanda's soul with sadness a little more each
time. It numbed Amanda, this sadness, and she knew she was
dying inside for her sins. She had resisted his advances at
first, even refusing big sums of money for her embroidery,
until one day, right before the full heat of the noon-day sun,
she remembered, he ceased his elaborate romantics, the offer-
ings, and guided her hand to his loin, hard like a stone, and
he rubbed her hand against it until he eased away, and she
realized she was rubbing of her own free will, without his
hand and she began to die.

When Don Joaquín pulled up her skirt, she heard the
music of the carousel. Chato, she sang to herself, over and

over, my lovely Chato, I miss you, your warmth, your scent, your love. Damn you, damn you, forgive and get on with our life, she thought over and over. But it was over; her marriage was over; now her affair with Don Joaquín would soon be over because guilt had grown into a cancer.

Her cheeks were sunken, he noticed, her hand trembled, when she told him goodbye. "As you wish," he replied without looking at her eyes. "But remember," pausing, the shock so great, "a dog is meaner when his paw is crushed." He rode off without stopping to see the progression of the workers, riding straight to the cantina where the woman waited with a mug of mescal, the dust making his eyes water with misery as he rode, his handkerchief crumbled up in his pocket, thinking Adiós, Amanda mía.

IV

The burden laid in carrying the mountain. Whether I travel paths on foot, my callouses as thick as leather, or ride on paved streets in a dirty bus, I have never seen myself moving. Because the mountain was too big for two little hands, one closed heart, too immovable. So finally after the long, long journey, keeping a pocket radio close, the static of the mountain sizzling in my ear, my lone companion except for the handkerchief, I must listen finally to the mountain's songs and sorrows before the gravel hits my face again. I face the mountain now only to realize—such blindness in me—that the mountain was no bigger than a stone, a stone I could have thrown into the distance where the earth and sky meet, thrown it away at twenty-four, but instead waited fifty-eight years later when Amanda returned, still damned, still grieving, still loving you, on the Day of the Dead, that day when all the veins of memories are pumped with the blood of resurrection so that finally, Amanda, you have returned superior to me and helped me to cast the stone, to bury it, and we will be reconciled for eternity; you and I, our children welcoming us at the entrance of the heartland.

It was a lie; the mountain was a stone; the carousel horse with a glossy silver saddle moving but going nowhere was just wood. Myself as a liberator was also a lie. Shortly after I left you standing on the porch, we both knew I was never returning. You stood there without a word, immovable as the mountain, watching me ride off on a borrowed cloud. Shortly after that I loved you more than when I first saw you standing in my room by the fire, and we both knew then all we ever needed to know. But our neighbors did not. They waved me like a flag of liberation, they watching me as you stood nailing my insides with your eyes, they saying to me, "if not for Pancha and the niños, I'd go fight with you." Me riding off to a different war, a different journey that was to end here in a city up north, Tejas, California, with tubes in my nose and arms where the federales would not hang me for murder. Maybe. Maybe to escape not from them but from you and your adultery. And yet I could never forget you, Amanda. After I left you, after I left the village, I lived for fifty-eight years but never saw life again. It began when I cheated you, drained you. You, in turn, cheated Don Joaquín. He cheated me and so I killed him. Maybe we were all born cheated. There is no justice, only honor in that little world out in the desert where our house sits like decayed bones. All that can be done is what you have done, Amanda; sit on the porch and weave your threads into time.

Snapshots

Snapshots

It was the small things in life, I admit, that made me happy: ironing straight-arrow creases on Dave's work khakis, cashing in enough coupons to actually save some money, or having my bus halt just right, so that I don't have to jump off the curb and crack my kneecap like that poor shoe salesman I read about in Utah. Now, it's no wonder that I wake mornings and try my damndest not to mimic the movements of ironing or cutting those stupid, dotted lines or slipping into my house shoes, groping for my robe, going to Marge's room to check if she's sufficiently covered, scruffling to the kitchen, dumping out the soggy coffee grounds, refilling the pot and only later realizing that the breakfast nook has been set for three, the iron is plugged in, the bargain page is open in front of me and I don't remember, I mean I really don't remember doing any of it because I've done it for thirty years now and Marge is already married. It kills me, the small things.

Like those balls of wool on the couch. They're small and senseless, and yet, every time I see them, I want to scream. Since the divorce, Marge brings me balls and balls and balls of wool thread because she insists that I "take up a hobby," "keep as busy as a bee," or "make the best of things," and all that other good-natured advice she probably hears from old folks who answer in such a way when asked how they've managed to live so long. Honestly, I wouldn't be surprised if she walked in one day with bushels of straw for me to weave into baskets. My only response to her endeavors is to give her the hardest stares I know how when she enters the living room, opens up her plastic shopping bag, and brings out another ball of bright-colored wool thread. I never move. Just sit and stare.

"Mother."

She pronounces the words not as a truth but as an accusation.

"Please, Mother. Knit. Do something." And then she places the new ball on top of the others on the couch, turns toward the kitchen and leaves. I give her a minute before I look out the window to see her standing on the sidewalk. I stick out my tongue, even make a face, but all she does is stand there with that horrible yellow and black plastic bag against her fat leg and wave good-bye.

Do something, she says. If I had a penny for all the things I have done, all the little details I was responsible for but which amounted to nonsense, I would be rich. But I haven't a thing to show for it. The human spider gets on prime-time television for climbing a building because its there. Me? How can people believe that I've fought against motes of dust for years or dirt attracting floors or perfected bleached-white sheets when a few hours later the motes, the dirt, the stains return to remind me of the uselessness of it all? I missed the sound of swans slicing the lake water or the fluttering wings of wild geese flying south for a warm winter or the heartbeat I could have heard if I had just held Marge a little closer.

I realize all that time is lost now, and I find myself searching for it frantically under the bed where the balls of dust collect undisturbed and untouched, as it should be.

To be quite frank, the fact of the matter is I wish to do nothing but allow indulgence to rush through my veins with frightening speed. I do so because I have never been able to tolerate it in anyone, including myself.

I watch television to my heart's content now, a thing I rarely did in my younger days. While I was growing up, television had not been invented. Once it was and became a must for every home, Dave saved and saved until we were able to get one. But who had the time? Most of mine was spent working part time as a clerk for Grants, then returning to create a happy home for Dave. This is the way I pictured it:

> His wife in the kitchen wearing a freshly ironed apron, stirring a pot of soup, whistling a whistle-while-you-work tune, and preparing frosting for some cupcakes so that when he drove home from work, tired and sweaty, he would enter his castle to find his cherub baby in a pink day suit with newly starched ribbons crawling to him and his wife looking at him with pleasing eyes and offering him a cupcake.

It was a good image I wanted him to have and everyday I almost expected him to stop, put down his lunch pail and cry at the whole scene. If it wasn't for the burnt cupcakes, my damn varicose veins, and Marge blubbering all over her day suit, it would have made a perfect snapshot.

Snapshots are ghosts. I am told that shortly after women are married, they become addicted to one thing or another. In *Reader's Digest* I read stories of closet alcoholic wives who gambled away grocery money or broke into their children's piggy banks in order to quench their thirst and fill their souls. Unfortunately, I did not become addicted to alcohol because my only encounter with it had left me senseless and with my face in the toilet bowl. After that, I never had the desire to repeat the performance of a senior in high school whose prom date never showed. I did consider my addiction a lot more incurable. I had acquired a habit much more deadly: nostalgia.

I acquired the habit after Marge was born and I had to stay in bed for months because of my varicose veins. I began flipping through my family's photo albums (my father threw them away after mom's death) to pass the time and pain away. However, I soon became haunted by the frozen moments and the meaning of memories. Looking at the old photos, I'd get real depressed over my second-grade teacher's smile or my father's can of beer or the butt-naked smile of me as a young teen, because every detail, as minute as it may seem, made me feel that so much had passed unnoticed. As a result, I began to convince myself that my best years were up and that I had nothing to look forward to. I was too young and too ignorant to realize that that section of my life relied wholly on those crumbling photographs and my memory, and I probably wasted more time longing for a past that never really existed. Dave eventually packed them up in a wooden crate to keep me from hurting myself. He was good in that way. Like when he clipped roses for me. He made sure the thorns were cut off so I didn't have to prick myself while putting them in a vase. And it was the same thing with the albums. They stood in the attic for years until I brought them down a day after he remarried.

The photo albums are unraveling and stained with spills and fingerprints and are filled with crinkled faded gray snapshots of people I can't remember anymore. I turn the pages

over and over again to see if somehow, some old dream will
come into my blank mind. Like the black and white television
box does when I turn it on. It warms up then flashes instant
pictures, instant lives, instant people.

Parents. That I know for sure. The woman is tall and
long, her plain black dress is over her knees, and she wears
thick spongelike shoes. She's over to the right of the photo,
looks straight ahead at the camera. The man wears white
baggy pants that go past his waist, thick suspenders. He
smiles while holding a dull-faced baby. He points to the camera. His sleeves are pulled up, his tie undor.e, his hair is
messy, as if some wild woman has driven his head between
her breasts and ran her fingers into his perfect, greased ducktail.

My mother always smelled of smoke and vanilla and that
is why I stayed away from her. I suppose that is why my
father stayed away from her as well. I don't ever remember a
time when I saw them show any sign of affection. Not like
today. No sooner do I turn off the soaps when I turn around
and catch two youngsters on a porch swing, their mouths
open, their lips chewing and chewing as if they were sharing
a piece of three-day-old liver. My mom was always one to
believe that such passion be restricted to the privacy of one's
house and then, there too, be demonstrated with efficiency
and not this urgency I witness almost every day. Dave and I
were good about that.

Whenever I saw the vaseline jar on top of Dave's bed-
stand, I made sure the door was locked and the blinds down.
This anticipation was more exciting to me than him lifting up
my flannel gown over my head, pressing against me, slipping
off my underwear then slipping into me. The vaseline came
next, then he came right afterwards. In the morning, Dave
looked into my eyes and I could never figure out what he
expected to find. Eventually, there came a point in our relationship when passion passed to Marge's generation, and I
was somewhat relieved. And yet, I could never imagine Marge
doing those types of things that these youngsters do today,
though I'm sure she did them on those Sunday afternoons
when she carried a blanket and a book and told me she was
going to the park to do some reading and returned hours later
with the bookmark in the same place. She must have done
them, or else how could she have gotten engaged, married,

had three children all under my nose, and me still going to check if she's sufficiently covered?

"Mother?" Marge's voice from the kitchen. It must be evening. Every morning it's the ball of wool, every evening it's dinner. Honestly, she treats me as if I have an incurable heart ailment. She stands under the doorway.

"Mother?" Picture it: She stands under the doorway looking befuddled, as if a movie director instructs her to stand there and look confused and upset; stand there as if you have seen your mother sitting in the same position for the last nine hours.

"What are you doing to yourself?" Marge is definitely not one for originality and she repeats the same lines every day. I'm beginning to think our conversation is coming from discarded scripts. I know the lines by heart, too. She'll say: "Why do you continue to do this to us?" and I'll answer: "Do what?" and she'll say: "This"—-waving her plump, coarse hands over the albums scattered at my feet—-and I'll say: "Why don't you go home and leave me alone?" This is the extent of our conversation and usually there is an optional line like: "I brought you something to eat," or "Let's have dinner," or "Come look what I have for you," or even "I brought you your favorite dish."

I think of the times, so many times, so many Mother's Days that passed without so much as a thank you or how sweet you are for giving us thirty years of your life. I know I am to blame. When Marge first started school, she had made a ceramic handprint for me to hang in the kitchen. My hands were so greasy from cutting the fat off some pork chops, I dropped it before I could even unwrap my first Mother's Day gift. I tried gluing it back together again with flour and water paste, but she never forgave me and I never received another gift until after the divorce. I wonder what happened to the ceramic handprint I gave to my mother?

In the kitchen I see that today my favorite dish is Chinese food getting cold in those little coffin-like containers. Yesterday my favorite dish was a salami sandwich, and before that a half-eaten rib, no doubt left over from Marge's half-hour lunch. Last week she brought me some Sunday soup that had fish heads floating around in some greenish broth. When I threw it down the sink, all she could think of to say was: "Oh, Mother."

We eat in silence. Or rather, she eats. I don't understand how she can take my indifference. I wish that she
would break out of her frozen look, jump out of any snapshot
and slap me in the face. Do something. Do something. I begin
to cry.

"Oh, Mother," she says, picking up the plates and putting
them in the sink.

"Mother, please."

There's fingerprints all over this one, my favorite. Both
woman and child are clones: same bathing suit, same pony-
tails, same ribbons. The woman is looking directly at the camera, but the man is busy making a sand castle for his
daughter. He doesn't see the camera or the woman. On the
back of this one, in vague pencil scratching, it says: San Juan
Capistrano.

This is a bad night. On good nights I avoid familiar spots.
On bad nights I am pulled towards them so much so that if I
sit on the chair next to Dave's I begin to cry. On bad nights I
can't sleep, and on bad nights I don't know who the couples in
the snapshots are. My mother and me? Me and Marge? I don't
remember San Juan Capistrano and I don't remember the
woman. She faded into thirty years of trivia. I don't even
remember what I had for dinner, or rather, what Marge had
for dinner, just a few hours before. I wrap a blanket around
myself and go into the kitchen to search for some evidence,
but except for a few crumbs on the table, there is no indication that Marge was here. Suddenly, I am relieved when I see
the box containers in the trash under the sink. I can't sleep
the rest of the night wondering what happened to my ceramic
handprint or what was in the boxes. Why can't I remember?
My mind thinks of nothing but those boxes in all shapes and
sizes. I wash my face with warm water, put cold cream on, go
back to bed, get up and wash my face again. Finally, I decide
to call Marge at 3:30 in the morning. The voice is faint and
there is static in the distance.

"Yes?" Marge asks automatically.

"Hello," Marge says. I almost expected her to answer her
usual "Dave's Hardware."

"Who is this?" Marge is fully awake now.

"What did we..." I ask, wondering why it was suddenly so
important for me to know what we had for dinner. "What did
you have for dinner?" I am confident that she'll remember

every movement I made or how much salt I put on whatever we ate, or rather, she ate. Marge is good about details.

"Mother?"

"Are you angry that I woke you up?"

"Mother. No. Of course not."

I could hear some muffled sounds, vague voices, static. I can tell she is covering the mouthpiece with her hand. Finally, George's voice.

"Mrs. Ruiz," he says, restraining his words so that they almost come out slurred, "Mrs. Ruiz, why don't you leave us alone?" and then there is a long buzzing sound. Right next to the vaseline jar are Dave's cigarettes. I light one though I don't smoke. I unscrew the jar and use the lid for an ashtray. I wait, staring at the phone until it rings.

"Dave's Hardware," I answer. "Don't you know what time it is?"

"Yes." It isn't Marge's voice. "Why don't you leave the kids alone?" Dave's voice is not angry. Groggy, but not angry. After a pause I say:

"I don't know if I should be hungry or not."

"You're a sad case." Dave says it as coolly as a doctor would say you have terminal cancer. He says it to convince me that it is totally out of his hands. I panic. I picture him sitting on his side of the bed in his shorts, smoking under a dull circle of light. I know his bifocals are down to the tip of his nose.

"Oh, Dave," I say. "Oh, Dave." The static gets worse.

"Let me call you tomorrow."

"No. Its just a bad night."

"Olga," Dave says so softly that I can almost feel his warm breath on my face. "Olga, why don't you get some sleep?"

The first camera I ever saw belonged to my grandfather. He won it in a cock fight. Unfortunately, he didn't know two-bits about it, but he somehow managed to load the film. Then he brought it over to our house. He sat me on the lawn. I was only five- or six-years old, but I remember the excitement of everybody coming around to get into the picture. I can see my grandfather clearly now. I can picture him handling the camera slowly, touching the knobs and buttons to find out how the camera worked while the men began milling around him expressing their limited knowledge of the invention. I remember it all so clearly. Finally, he was able to manage the camera and he took pictures of me standing near my mother with the wives behind us.

My grandmother was very upset. She kept pulling me out of the picture, yelling to my grandfather that he should know better, that snapshots steal the souls of the people and that she would not allow my soul to be taken. He pushed her aside and clicked the picture.

The picture, of course, never came out. My grandfather, not knowing better, thought that all he had to do to develop the film was unroll it and expose it to the sun. After we all waited for an hour, we realized it didn't work. My grandmother was very upset and cut a piece of my hair, probably to save me from a bad omen.

It scares me to think that my grandmother may have been right. It scares me even more to think I don't have a snapshot of her. If I find one, I'll tear it up for sure.

Neighbors

Neighbors

I

Aura Rodríguez always stayed within her perimeters, both personal and otherwise, and expected the same of her neighbors. She was quite aware that the neighborhood had slowly metamorphosed into a graveyard. People of her age died off only to leave their grandchildren with little knowledge of struggle. As a result, the children gathered near her home in small groups to drink, to lose themselves in the abyss of defeat, to find temporary solace among each other. She shared the same streets and corner stores and midnights with these tough-minded young men who threw empty beer cans into her yard, but once within her own solitude, surrounded by a tall wrought-iron fence, she belonged to a different time. Like those who barricaded themselves against an incomprehensible generation, Aura had resigned herself to live with the caution and silence of an apparition, as she had lived for the past seventy-three years, asking no questions, assured of no want, no deep-hearted yearning other than to live out the remainder of her years without hurting anyone, including herself.

And so it came as no surprise that when a woman appeared on a day much like every day, Aura continued sweeping her porch, oblivious to what her neighbors had stopped in mid-motion to watch.

The massive woman with a vacuous hole of a mouth entered Bixby Street, a distinct scent accompanying her. She was barefooted and her feet, which were cracked, dirty, and encrusted with dry blood, were impossible to imagine once babysmall and soft. The woman carried her belongings in two soiled brown bags. Her mouth caved into a smile as the neighbors watched her black cotton wig flop to one side. They stared at her huge breasts, sagging like sacks of sand and wobbling with every limp. Mrs. García pinched her nose as the woman passed, and Toastie, washing his candied-apple red Impala, threatened to hose her down. Aura stopped sweeping her porch and leaned on her broomstick, not to stare at the woman's badly mended dress or her wig that glistened with caked hairspray, but to watch the confident direction she took, unmoved by the taunts and stares. Aura did something she had not done in a while: she smiled. However, when the woman stopped at her gate, Aura's smile evaporated. Haphazardly, the woman placed one bag down in order to scratch beneath her wig.

"Doña Aura Rodríguez," she said finally, her toothless mouth collapsing with each word, making it difficult for Aura to understand. "Where is Señor Macario Fierro de Ortega? Where is he?"

"Macario Fierro de Ortega?" Aura repeated the name as she stepped down her porch steps hesitantly, dragging the broom behind her. Fierro had lived behind her house for nearly thirty years, but she had never known his full name. Perhaps she was not referring to *her* Fierro.

"Señor Macario Fierro de Ortega?" she asked, eyeing the woman suspiciously. Aura knew of at least four ways of describing the smell of neglected flesh, but none seemed adequate to describe what stood in front of her. The woman became nervous under Aura's scrutiny. She began rummaging through her bags like one looking for proof of birth at a border crossing, and found what she had been looking for. Pinching the corner of the matchbook cover, Aura read the barely visible scribbling: 1306 1/2 Bixby Street. It was Fierro's address, all right. She returned the matchbook and eyed the woman, all the while debating what to do. The woman was indeed a massive presence, but although she overshadowed Aura's small, delicate frame, the whites of her eyes were as vague as old memories. Hard years had etched her chapped and sunburnt face. It was because of this that Aura finally said: "In the back," and she pointed to a small weather-worn house. "But he's not home. On Tuesdays they give ten-cent lunches at the center." The woman's scent made it unbearable to stand near her for long, and Aura politely stepped back.

"Who cares?" The woman laughed, crumbling the matchbook and tossing it behind her shoulder. "Waiting I know how to do!" She unhinged the gate and limped into Aura's yard, her scent following like a cloud of dust.

Aura was confused as she returned to her house. Her memory swelled with old stories which began with similar circumstances, and she began to worry about being duped. As she opened the door to a cluttered room, one thing struck her as strange, so she drew the Venetian blinds and locked the door behind her: how did the woman know her name?

II

Dressed in his Saturday sharpest, Chuy finished the last of his beer behind the Paramount Theater before meeting Laura in the balcony, "the dark side." When he threw the *tall dog* into a huge trash bin, three men jumped the alley wall and attacked him. As they struck at him, he managed to grab a 2 by 4 which was holding the trash lid open. But it was no match for the switchblade which ripped through his chest. Chuy was nineteen when Fierro identified the body. He slowly pried the 2 by 4 from his son's almost womanly slender fingers and carried the blood-stained plank of wood home with him. Years and years later, as his legs grew as feeble as his mind, he took the 2 by 4 from his closet and sat on Aura's porch, whittling a cane for himself and murmuring to his son as she watered her beloved rose bushes, chinaberry tree, and gardenias.

The neighbors, of course, thought him crazy. Pabla from across the street insisted that talking to a dead son was an indication of senility. But others swore on their grandmother's grave that he or she saw Chuy sitting on Aura's porch, combing his hair "the way they used to comb it then." Although each aired their opinion of Fierro's son while waiting in the checkout line at the First Street Store, everyone agreed on one thing: Fierro was strangely touched. The fact that no one, not even the elderly Castillos could remember his first name, added to the mystery of the man. The butcher with the gold tooth, the priest at the Virgen de Guadalupe Church, and the clerk who collected the money for his Tuesday ten-cent lunch addressed him as Don Fierro. But behind his back everyone shook their head with pity.

All the neighbors, that is, except Aura. Throughout the years of sharing the same front gate, a silent bond between the two sprouted and grew firmer and deeper with time. As a result, he alone was allowed to sit on her porch swing as he whittled. With sad sagging eyes and whiskey breath, he described for hours his mother's face and the scent of wine grapes just before harvest. He often cried afterwards and returned home in quiet shame, closing his door discreetly. Aura would continue her watering into the evening, until she saw the light in his kitchen flick on. Then she was sure that he was now sober enough to fix himself something to eat. Not until he had finished whittling the cane did he stop sitting on Aura's porch.

With the help of his cane, Fierro walked home from the Senior Citizen Center Luncheon. He coughed up some phlegm, then spit it out in disgust. Eating was no longer a pleasure for him; it was as distasteful as age. The pale, salt-less vegetables, the crumbling beef and the warm milk were enough to make any man vomit. Whatever happened to the real food, the beans with cheese and onions and chile, the flour tortillas? Once again he did what he had done every Tuesday for the last five years: he cursed himself for having thrown away priceless time.

He walked with great difficulty, and when he reached the freeway on-ramp crossing, he paused to catch his breath. The cars and trucks and motorcycles, in their madness to reach an unknown destination, flung past him onto the freeway, caus-ing his green unbuttoned vest to flap open. With his free hand he held the rim of his gray fedora. Fierro slowly began his trek across the on-ramp while the truckers honked impa-tiently.

"Cabrones!" he yelled, waving his cane indignantly, "I hope you live to be my age!" And he continued his walk, turn-ing off his hearing aid so that the sounds in his head were not the sirens or motors or horns, but the sounds of a seashell pressed tightly against his ear. When he finally reached the freeway overpass, he stood there listening to the absence of sound.

"Fierro, Don Fierro!" A young woman and her daughter stood in front of him. He saw the young child retreat behind her mother's skirt, frightened by the ancient face. "Don Fierro, are you all right?" The woman shouted over her gro-cery bag and into his ear. He remembered to turn on his hearing aid, and when he did, he heard her ask, "Are you all right?!"

"Heartaches," he said finally, shaking his head. "Incurable. It's a cancer that lays dormant only to surprise you when you least expect it."

"What could it be?" the young woman asked as she went into her bag and busted a chip of chicharrón. Loosening her grip on her mother's apron, the child took the chicharrón and chewed loudly, sucking the fat.

"Memories," Fierro said.

He heard the sirens again, the swift traffic whirling by beneath him. He was suddenly amazed how things had changed and how easy it would be to forget that there were once quiet hills here, hills that he roamed until they were flattened into vacant lots where dirt paths became streets and houses became homes. Then the government letter arrived and everyone was forced to uproot, one by one, leaving behind rows and rows of wooden houses that creaked with swollen age. He remembered, realizing as he watched the carelessness with which the company men tore into the shabby homes with clawing efficiency, that it was easy for them to demolish some twenty, thirty, forty years of memories within a matter of months. As if that weren't enough, huge pits were dug to make sure that no roots were left. The endless freeway paved over his sacred ruins, his secrets, his graves, his fertile soil in which all memories were seeded and waiting for the right time to flower, and he could do nothing.

He could stand right where he was standing now and say to himself, here was where the Paramount Theater stood, and over there I bought snow cones for the kids, here was where Chuy was stabbed, over there the citrus orchards grew. He knew it would never be the same again, never, and his greatest fear in life, greater than his fear of death or of not receiving his social-security check, was that he would forget so much that he would not know whether it was like that in the first place, or whether he had made it up, or whether he had made it up so well that he began to believe it was true. He looked down at the child munching on the last of the chicharrón. I remember when you were that age, he wanted to say to the woman. But he was not sure anymore, he was not sure if he did. With his swollen, blotched hands, he tipped his gray fedora, then patted her hands softly.

"I'll be just fine," he reassured her, taking a last look at
the child. "It's Tuesday," he said finally, and turning off his
hearing aid once again, he prepared himself for the long walk
across the ruins that still danced with Chuy's ghost.

III

When she heard the gate open, Aura's first impulse was
to warn Fierro of the woman who had been sitting on his
porch for the last two hours. But since she respected him too
much to meddle in his affairs, she went to the back room of
her house and did something else she hadn't done in a long
time: she peaked through her washroom window.

Contrary to her expectations, Fierro was not at all bewildered or surprised. He stood there, leaning on his cane while
the woman rose from the porch with difficulty. They ex-
changed a few words. When Aura saw Fierro dig into his
pocket, it infuriated her to think that the woman had come
for money. But instead of producing his wallet, he brought out
his keys and opened the door. The woman entered majesti-
cally while a pigeon on his porch awning cooed at her arrival.

IV

There was a group of pigeons on Fierro's awning by
morning, and it was the cooing and not the knock that awoke
her. Aura finally sat up, the familiar ache of her swollen feet
pulsating, and with one twisted finger guided a Ben Gay-
scented house slipper onto each foot. She leaned against the
wall as she walked to the door, her bones, joints and the mus-
cles of her legs and feet throbbing under the weight of her
body. By the time she got to the door, no one was there. Aura
retreated to her room, leaning from chair to table, from couch
to wall. Her legs folded under her as she collapsed on the bed.

By evening she had tried almost everything to rid herself
of the pain, and her lips were parched with bitterness. Miserable and cornered, she began cursing her body, herself for
such weakness. She slept little, rocking her head helplessly
against the pillow as the pain continued to crawl up and down
her body. She began to hate. She hated her body, the ticking
of the hen-shaped clock which hung above the stove and the
way the dogs howled at the police sirens. She hated the way

her fingers distorted her hand so that she could not even grasp a glass of water. But most of all she hated the laughter and the loud music which came from the boys who stood around the candied-apple red Impala with the tape deck on full blast. They laughed and drank and threw beer cans in her yard while she burned with fever. The pain finally made her so desperate with intolerance that she struggled to her porch steps, tears moistening her eyes, and pleaded with the boys.

"Por favor," she said, her feeble plea easily swallowed up by the blast of an oldie. "Don't you have homes?"

"What?" Toastie asked, not moving from where he stood.

"Go home," she pleaded, leaning against a porch pillar, her legs folding under her. "Go home. Go home."

"We *are* home!" Rubén said while opening another malt liquor. The others began to laugh. She held herself up because the laughter echoed in her head and she refused to be mocked by these little men who knew nothing of life and respect. But she slipped and fell and they continued to laugh. It was their laughter at her inability to even stand on her own two feet that made her call the police.

She raged with fever and revenge, waiting for the police to arrive. She tipped the slats of the Venetian blinds to watch the boys standing in a circle passing a joint, each savoring the sweet taste of the marihuana cigarette as they inhaled. She remembered Toastie as a child. She had even witnessed his baptism, but now he stood tall and she wondered where he had learned to laugh so cruelly. She lowered her head. The world was getting too confusing now, so that you even had to call the police in order to get some kindness from your neighbors.

Her feeling of revenge had overcome her pain momentarily, but when the police arrived, she fully realized her mistake. The five cars zeroed in on their target, halting like tanks in a cartoon. The police jumped out in military formation, ready for combat. The neighbors began emerging from behind their doors and fences to watch the red lights flashing against the policemen's batons. When the boys were lined up, spreadeagled for the search, Toastie made a run for it, leaping over Aura's wrought-iron fence and falling hard on a rose bush. His face scratched and bleeding, he ran towards her door, and for a moment Aura was sure he wanted to kill her. It was not until he lunged for the door that she was able to see the desperation and confusion, the fear in his eyes, and he screamed at the top of his lungs while pounding on her door, the *vowels* of the one word melting into a howl, he screamed to her, "Pleeeeeeease."

He pounded on the door. "Please!" She pressed her hands against her ears until his howl was abruptly silenced by a dull thud. When the two policemen dragged him down the porch steps, she could hear the creak of their thick leather belts rubbing against their bullets. She began to cry.

It was not until way into the night, after she locked each window, each door, after her neighbors had retreated behind their T.V.s leaving her alone once again, that she remembered the last thing Rubén yelled as the patrol cars drove off, the last words he said as he struggled with the handcuffs.

"We'll get you," he said. "You'll see."

V

For several days the brooding clouds began to form into animal and plant shapes until they finally burst, pelting her windows with rain. Fearful of her light bulbs attracting lightning, she turned them off and was content to sit in the dark next to the stove while the gas burners flickered blue and yellow fire upon the wall. She sat there quietly with a quilt over her shoulders, her shadow a wavering outline of a woman intimidated by natural forces. Aura sat and listened to the monotony of seconds, the thunderclaps, the pelting against her windows. It was only after the rain had subsided that a faint nasal melody playing against a rusty needle penetrated her darkness, and she cocked her head to listen. Aura carried her chair to the washroom window. She seated herself, pulled up the Venetian blind slats and sought the source of the music.

The music was faint, barely an audible tune, but she recognized it just the same. She pressed her face against the coldness of the window glass and tried to remember why the song seemed so familiar. The Hallmark dance floor. She remembered the Hallmark dance floor and smiled. The toilet tank had been broken, and for a few dollars, plus tips, she was hired to fill buckets of water and pour them in the tank after every flush. She was thirteen years old, and the manager, a round stout man who wore a bulky gold diamond ring on his small finger, warned her against peaking out the door. She remembered sitting next to the sinks with her buckets full, tapping her feet to the rhythm of the music, as she did now, listening intently. And she imagined, as she imagined then, the prism ball encircling the couples with pieces of diamond specks. She recalled the glitter, the laughter, conversations, the thick level of cigarette smoke which hovered over the dancers so that it seemed they were dancing in clouds. It was nice to hear the laughter again, and mist collected on the window from her slow breathing. As night filtered in, Aura made out a silhouette against the shade of Fierro's room, and she recognized the massive shape immediately. The woman was dancing, slow lazy movements like those of a Sunday summer breeze teasing a field of tall grass. She held a scarf and slowly manipulated it as though it were a serpent. Fierro was laughing. The laugh was an unfamiliar sound to Aura's ears, as if a screw had loosened somewhere inside his body and began to rattle. But he continued to laugh a laugh that came from deep within and surfaced to express a genuine enjoyment of living.

Aura felt like an intruder, peering into their bedroom window and witnessing their intimacy. Although she hated herself for spying, she could not pry herself away from the window, away from the intimacies, away from the tune she had buried so far down that she had forgotten its existence. She listened way into the night, keeping the rhythm of the music with her foot, until the record finished with a scratch and Aura went to bed, cold under the bleached, white sheets.

VI

Aura was in the mood to dance, to loosen her inhibitions from the tight confines of shoes and explore a barefoot freedom she had never experienced in her wakeful hours. But she awoke to stare at her feet, to inspect the swelling, to let reality slowly sink in, and she was thankful and quite satisfied simply to be able to walk.

She dressed slowly because she felt weak and uneasy, and at first attributed the hollowness of her stomach to the medication she had taken throughout those endless nights. But when she lifted the blinds to the washroom window and saw the woman standing barefoot on the porch, tossing bread crumbs to the pigeons while her bracelets clinked with every toss, Aura knew it was not the medication. She watched the woman scratch beneath her huge breasts while she yawned, then turn towards the door, closing it with a loud slam. Aura's heart sank like an anchor into an ocean of silence. She drew the blinds quietly.

In the kitchen Aura flipped up the lid of the coffee can, spooned the grinds into the percolator, dropped in a stick of cinnamon, and put the pot to boil. When the coffee was done, she poured herself a cup. It was bitter, and the more she thought about the woman, the more bitter the coffee became. She heard the children of Bixby Street, who were especially happy to see the storm pass. Having been imprisoned by the rains, they were now freed from behind their doors and allowed to run the streets under the bright sun. Aura heard their shouts, their laughter, and she yearned to feel right again.

She collected a sunbonnet, gloves and garden tools. Since the rainfall had soaked the soil, she could not pass up the opportunity to weed out her garden, and even though her movements were sluggish, she prepared herself for a day's work.

Once outside and under the bright sun, Aura was blinded for a moment. She bit her fist in disbelief. Most of the graffiti was sprayed on her front porch with black paint, but some of it was written with excrement. As she slowly stepped down, she inspected the windows, steps, walkway, pillars, all defaced with placas, symbols, vulgarities. She rushed over the chayote vine and made a feeble attempt to replant it, but everything, her flowers, chayotes, gardenias, rose bushes, were uprooted and cast aside. Some of her bushes were twenty years old, having begun as cuttings from her mother's garden. She had spent years guiding and pruning and nurturing them until they blossomed their gratitude. She tried unsuccessfully to restore them, the thorns scratching her face, her bare hands bleeding. When she fell to her knees and began clawing away at the mud in hopes of saving some of her bushes, she failed to notice that the children had stopped their play and stood in front of her yard, their red, puffy faces peering from between her wrought-iron bars. It was their look of bewilderment and pity that made her realize the hopelessness of her actions.

"Leave me alone!" Aura screamed at the children, raising her arms like a menacing bird. "Leave me alone or I'll...," she shouted, and the children scattered in all directions like cockroaches. She stood up, her knees trembling, and took one last look at her plants. All that remained intact was her chinaberry tree. Aura slowly returned to the house, her hands dangling uselessly at her side. "I'm so glad," she thought, fighting back the tears as the mutilated bushes began shriveling under the morning sun. "I'm so glad I'm going to die soon."

She closed the door behind her, made sure all the locks were locked, unrolled the Venetian blinds, closed the drapes. She heard Rubén's voice: "We'll get you." Picking up the phone, she decided against calling the police and making another mistake. Fierro? She was totally alone. "We'll get you, you'll see." She would have to take care of herself. She was marked, proof to other neighbors that indeed the "BIXBY BOYS RULE," as they had sprayed the neighborhood in huge bold letters. NO. She refused to be their sacrificial lamb. She shook her head as she got a candlestick out of the linen closet. She pushed the kitchen table aside, grunting under its weight, then rolled up the carpet. She lit the candlestick and opened the cellar door because she refused to be helpless.

Cupping the faint flicker of the candle, she slowly descended into the gut of the cellar, grasping at the spider webs which blocked the way to her destination. She ignored the distorted shadows of the undisturbed furniture, ignored the scent of moistened, decayed years, and moved towards the pile of boxes stacked in the corner. She opened the first box with little difficulty, the motes of dust dancing around her until they settled once again to begin a new accumulation of years. She dug her hands into the box, groping, feeling beneath the objects, kitchen utensils, books, photographs, but found nothing. She threw the box aside and opened another. And another. With each box her anger and desperation rose so that the search became frantic, almost obsessive. Finally, in the last of the boxes, her fingers froze to the cool touch. She blew the dust away and examined it like the foreign object that it was. It felt cold and clumsy in her small hand. Nonetheless, she triumphantly placed the gun in her apron pocket and blew out the last of the candlestick.

VII

As the days passed, Fierro knew little of what went on in the neighborhood. When he heard the sirens and screams and CB radios spitting out messages, he refused to go outside for fear of finding Chuy's body limp and bloody once again. Then, this morning as he turned from his side of the bed to examine the woman's slow breathing, he couldn't imagine what had caused Aura to scream so loudly that it startled him out of a sleepy daze, though he wore no hearing aid. All that Fierro knew was that he awoke one morning to find the warm mass of a woman sleeping beside him, and this was enough to silence any curiosity. He also knew never to ask a question if he wasn't prepared for the answer, and so he was content to let her stay for as long as she wanted without even asking her name.

Fierro sat up in bed, rubbed his eyes, palmed his hair back, yawned the last of his sleep away. As though in thoughtful meditation, he allowed his body to slowly return to consciousness, allowed the circulation to drive away the numbness from his limbs. Only then was he ready to make the walk across the room to the bathroom. He winced as he walked on the cold floor, and he took one last look at the woman before he closed the door.

Inside the bathroom, Fierro urinated, washed his hands and face in cool water, inspected the day's growth of beard in the mirror. He rinsed his dentures under running water, then slipped them into his mouth, clacking his jaws twice to make sure they fell securely in place. Not until he had almost finished his shave did it occur to him that he had been humming. While he stood in front of the mirror, his raspy voice vibrated a tune. A ballroom-dancing, nice-smelling-women tune. He hummed louder as he shook some Wildroot into his hands and palmed his hair a second time. He combed it into a glossy ducktail, smoothed his mustache, smiled. He was about to slap on some cologne when Chuy stopped him.

"Can I do it," his young son asked eagerly. As he had done every morning, the boy stood on the toilet seat to watch his father's daily shave. He was small and thin, and the crotch of his underwear hung to his knees. "Can I?" Chuy repeated.

The boy had great respect for the daily shave. He would watch his father maneuver the single blade across his cheek with the same admiration he felt watching a performer swallow a sword. But Chuy knew that, unlike sword swallowing, shaving would be accessible if only he studied it with the watchful eye of an apprentice. So it was a ritual each morning to spend the time necessary to stare at the blade, apply the cologne, and touch his own cheek for hair growth.

"Ay, qué Mi'jo. ¿Por qué no?" Fierro poked his son's belly with the bottle. He handed it to Chuy and tugged up his calzones. While the boy shook a few drops onto his palm, Fierro noticed how dirty his son's fingernails were. He would bathe him when he returned home.

"Ready?" Chuy asked. He kept his eyes on the palm of his hand, then when Fierro was close enough, he slapped his father's face as hard as he could. Fierro's exaggerated wince made the boy laugh.

"Now your turn." The boy enjoyed this part of the ritual because his father's scent would be with him all day. Fierro shook the scented rose water onto his cement-burned hand. But time had a way of passing so that the few seconds it took to shake out some of his son's favorite cologne turned into years, and the admiration in the boy's eyes had disappeared.

"I'm 19. I think I can do it myself." Fierro felt the rose water dripping through his fingers. It seemed like only yesterday... The bathroom seemed too small now, and they both elbowed one another. Fierro finally won over the mirror, but the defeat did not keep Chuy from trying to catch a glimpse of himself from behind his father's shoulders.

"Where do you think you're going?" Fierro asked, looking at Chuy's reflection, his face threatening a mustache. The answer was automatic: "Out."

"Don't get smart, Chuy." Fierro was becoming increasingly disturbed that Chuy was running the streets. "Hijo, you're not a dog. You have a home to live, to sleep, to eat in."

"Listen, Jefe," Chuy replied, tired of the same Saturday-night dialogue. "I'm old enough to know what I'm doing."

"Then why don't you act like it?"

"Shit, Jefe. Lay off for once."

"Qué lay off, ni qué ojo de hacha," Fierro replied angrily. "And don't be using that language with me, you understand?" There was an icy silence. Chuy combed his hair back. He waited patiently for the right time to break the silence and still save face. Finally: "Listen, Apá. I'm not going cruising, if that's what you want to know."

Fierro thought for a moment. Finally: "Good, mijito. Good. It's just that those chavalos are a bunch of good-for-nothings. Thieves. Murderers and thieves."

"You forgot tecatos."

"That, too."

"They're my friends."

"Bah! Qué friends! Look what they did to the Reyes boy."

Chuy bent over to smooth out the creases of his khaki pants, unconcerned by the accusation. When he looked up, he was face to face with his father. Barely whispering he said, "He had it coming to him."

"Do you really, really believe that?" In disbelief he looked into his son's eyes and realized how little he really knew him. How could anyone deserve to be murdered? It grieved him to think that Chuy was no different than the rest. But he was; Chuy, his son, his boy, had a good heart, and that made him different. Bad ways, but a good heart. Chuy defiantly returned his father's stare until his face broke into a smile.

"Apá," he said, slapping his father on the shoulder, "are you gonna lend me the cologne or what?" He rubbed each shoe against his pant leg. His shoulders were now stooped so that he was no longer taller than his father. "Laura and me, we're gonna go to a movie."

"Ay, qué, mi'jo!" Fierro was relieved. Get him out of the neighborhood. That much he knew if he wanted to save his son's good heart. He slapped the cologne on both sides of Chuy's face. "Ay, qué mi'jo. Laura and you!" The woman pounded on the door. "Got your key, mi'jo? And don't forget to lock the door after..."

"Ay te watcho, Jefito," Chuy interrupted. Taking a last look at his reflection, he winked at his father and was gone.

The woman pounded on the door again and Fierro opened it. She handed him the hearing aid, and, after a few adjustments, he was able to hear. As he followed her into the kitchen, he wanted to tell her about Chuy. But once he caught the aroma of the beans, he immediately forgot what he had wanted to say.

The woman grated some cheese, then sprinkled it on the boiling beans. After the cheese had melted, she spooned the beans onto the flour tortillas. Fierro ate the burritos as greedily as the pigeons pecked their crumbs of bread outside. As he licked his fingers, she poured some instant coffee into his tin cup then added some milk and honey. His hands trembled whenever he lifted the cup to his lips, sipping loudly.

"Good," he finally said. "It's all so good," and he reached over the table to touch her hand. As he had done for the past several days, Fierro studied her face, the crevices and creases, the moles and marks, studied those things which distinguish one person from another in hopes of finding something which would deliver immediate recognition. But in the end, as always, his mind became exhausted, and once again he failed. Beads of perspiration formed on the temples of his forehead, and the room began to circle and circle around him.

"Macario!?" the woman asked. But before he could answer, he fainted. Kneeling beside him, she looked around the room in confusion and fear, hoping to find something that would revive him and make him well. But all she could do, all she could think of, was to get the dishcloth and place it on his forehead. He began to squirm. Finally, when he was semi-conscious, he whispered to her, his lips feeling heavy and swollen, "Heartaches."

She helped him to the bed, pulling the blankets aside, and he slipped into sleep, smelling her scent in the sheets. He slept for a while, dreaming of watermelons so cool and refreshing to his lips, until the first abdominal cramp hit and he groped around for her hand. He wanted to ask for water, but his lips were swollen and dried and he couldn't speak. He was extremely thirsty and craved melons: crenshaw melons, honeydew melons, cantaloupe melons, watermelons. The woman bathed him in cool water, but the water could not extinguish the burning in his mouth and stomach. A second spasm hit without warning, his whole body cramping into a fetal position. With the onset of the third spasm, the retching began.

The woman became frantic and paced around and around his bed like a caged lioness. He was dying and she couldn't do anything because he had already made up his mind, and she wrung and wrung her hands in helplessness. When she finally picked up the phone, Fierro, barely able to move, motioned with his finger NO, then pointed to a chair. The hours passed as she sat next to him, rocking herself back and forth, mesmerized in deep prayer.

His lips were parched but his craving for coolness suddenly disappeared. He turned to look at the woman and finally, after some time, finally, recognized her. Before he could say her name again, he felt an avalanche crush his chest and he could no longer breathe. Fierro desperately inhaled in hopes of catching some air, but the more desperate he became, the less he could breathe. In short fits of spasms, his life snapped.

The pillow fell to her feet and she gently lifted his head to replace it. She tried to arouse him, but he lay still, his eyes yellow and dull. She pressed her ear against his chest. There was no breathing, no heartbeat, just a faint buzzing sound. The woman shook her head sadly as she slowly reached into his shirt pocket and turned off the hearing aid. She began moaning. At first light, and hardly audible, her moaning began to crescendo into high wails of sorrow and disbelief. Shrieking angrily at the God who convinced Fierro to die, the barefooted woman ran out, the screen door slamming behind her.

VIII

With her heart beating in a maddening race, Aura sat facing the front door, the gun on her lap. Her sunbonnet still hung limply by the side of her head, and her hands and face were smeared with dry blood and mud. The hours came and went with the ticking of the clock, and she waited, cocking the gun whenever she heard car brakes, her fear swelling to her throat, then releasing the trigger and relaxing once the car had spun away.

The summer of the rattlers. The Vizcano Desert was far away, yet she could almost feel the rattlers coiled up under the brittle bushes waiting for her. As a child she was frightened by their domination of the desert. If they were disturbed, they struck with such force that it was always too late to do anything. Her grandfather had taught her how to look for them, how to avoid them, and if necessary, how to kill them. But the sight of one always made her immobile because she had no protection against their menacing appearance, their slickness as they slowly slithered to a cooler location, or their instinct to survive. And so she never left the house without grandfather. But he was dead, and she would be soon if she didn't protect herself. Her eyes grew heavy with sleep but she refused to close them, for the rattlers were out there. Somewhere.

Aura finally dozed, her head falling forward until the loud door slam startled her into wakefulness and she groped around for the gun. She could not keep her body from trembling as she stood up from her chair to listen to the sounds coming from outside. She heard running footsteps, panting, and she felt the sweat dripping between her breasts. Someone was on her porch and she prayed to be left alone. She held the gun high with both hands, squeezing, tightly squeezing it as she aimed at the door.